Wintertime Journeys
with Different Kinds of Holidays

Boxing Day at Wentworth Manor brings joy and celebration.
But a cruel crime threatens to ruin the party

A heartless theft nearly breaks the spirit of Jennifer's family.
So she and her best friend set out to make things right.

The Christmas season hits hard for some people.
Yet it sometimes also brings hope for recovery and renewal.

June and Ryan share a ritual of grief and letting go.
Will their instant spark light the way to new possibilities?

Carrie faces Christmas in a new city.
Then she finds a true family to join for the celebration.

Virginia lived a long, joyful life. Full of family and love.
But her most cherished story remains untold.

Stuart's Stop 'N Shop, always open, even for Christmas.
Then the holiday spirit surprises Stuart, Bobby, and Pete.

Henry and Steve get caught by a Christmas Eve blizzard.
Will they grab their chance for happily ever after?

Collections:

Fantastic Shorts: Volume 1

Fantastic Shorts: Volume 2

Fantastic Shorts: Volume 3

Escape into Romance

Stepping Out of Reality

Facing Down Extraordinary

Hacking Cybercrime

Investigations Beyond Belief

Passages in the Real World

Fantastic Side Trips

A Kaleidoscope of Cat Tales

A Tapestry of Holiday Tales

Aunties Among Us

Four-Legged Heroes

Anthologies *with Jason A. Adams*:

Partners in Romance

Shadows Mountain Deep

Partnership in Crime

More great reads from Jason A. Adams

www.JasonAdamsBooks.com

Novellas:

Agonist

Collections and Anthologies:

Normally Fantastic

On the Case!

Capeless Heroes

Through the Squirrel Tree

Tales From the Squirrel Garden: Volume 1

(with Kari Kilgore)

Partners in Romance

Partnership in Crime

Shadows Mountain Deep

Near Future Forward

JASON A.
ADAMS
KARI
KILGORE

Uncommon Holidays

Spiral Publishing, Ltd.

Uncommon Holidays:
A Different Side of the Season

Published 2025 by Spiral Publishing, Ltd.
www.SpiralPublishing.net

ISBN-13: 978-1-63992-015-0
Digital ISBN-13: 978-1-63992-074-7
Large Print ISBN-13: 978-1-63992-016-7
Hardcover ISBN-13: 978-1-63992-017-4

For everyone who views the winter holidays
in their own joyful light

CONTENTS

NOT YOUR TYPICAL CELEBRATION

KARI KILGORE AND JASON A. ADAMS

Kari:

I've always been drawn to unconventional things. Whether it was clothing, music, or the books I read, I've never been one to make sure I'm always going along with the crowd.

That's not to say I force myself away from something I like simply because it's popular. There are times when I love the number one bestseller or that buzzy TV series. And my favorite sweatpants, t-shirt, and hoodie combination is hardly unusual, certainly not in the early years of the 2020s.

But more often than not, I'm a little off-center in my tastes.

The North American winter holidays, especially during the madness of the run-up to Christmas, are certainly no exception.

My husband Jason and I had a Christmas tree

one time, not long after we first moved in together. Watching our kitten bat ornaments out from her perch in the middle of the tree combined with seeing our puppy grab a garland and run as hard as he could with it convinced us both to end that tradition right there.

Our current holiday tree lineup—thirty years after that first tree disaster—is a two-foot version of the poor little tree from *A Charlie Brown Christmas*, the same size tree from *A Nightmare Before Christmas*, and a bright orange Halloween tree. I know that last one is hardly a winter holiday. But since we leave all three of them out year-round, that doesn't make all that much difference.

When it comes to writing holiday stories, the toddler who runs the writing machine in my head has a similarly off-kilter taste. Even when I write during the typical season, odds are high I'm going to come at it in an odd way.

Not just to be different, though I don't mind that end result one bit. In fact, I've written more than one holiday romance story that could be called totally mainstream, and I love those just as much. Looking for a different approach is more to keep that toddler—and myself—interested and excited about telling that particular story.

That's the true secret of writing, at least for me. Find a way to make each story fun.

Or at least strange enough to get me intrigued.

Another approach that draws my creative side into a story is finding a different experience, or a different mood. It can be so easy to assume everyone is having the same kind of holiday, especially for one so visible and dominant as Christmas in the United States.

Of course the truth is many people celebrate other holidays during that time of year, or they don't celebrate at all. Or they choose to observe the typical holidays in a non-traditional way.

Some gather with families of their own making, for enough reasons to keep me writing for the rest of my days.

Many people are still part of the mainstream, at least from the outside. But any number of circumstances could push them into an unusual mindset, an emotional place that's entirely out of step with the world around them.

Those are the kinds of stories in *Uncommon Holidays*. They're a bit different, and hopefully they'll give you exactly the type of escape you need when all the usual trappings and music and obligations turn out to be a bit much.

My first story, *Pungent Justice*, visits a family doing their best to look normal from the outside as Christmas approaches. But on the inside, unwanted changes have taken a toll. Then what seems like the last cruel straw pushes Jennifer into taking action. Her best friend and secret-identity ally Lynda is all too happy to cooperate. Sometimes, even during the holidays, what you really need is sweet, and pungent, revenge.

In *Finding Sanctuary*, I wanted to write about a different December holiday, and even then, find my own way into the story. The winter solstice, or the first day of winter, is fairly well-known in itself, and one with a lot of meaning for me. But I didn't want to dig into that just yet. Instead I found a newer tradition called Longest Night. The idea of taking that time—when the sun and its warmth and light are distant—and using it as a ritual for healing makes so much sense to me. Acknowledging changes good or bad, and sitting with what they mean. Making a decision to move forward even when it hurts.

I wrote this story in late 2019, during what seems like such an innocent time in retrospect. It was published as part of WMG Publishing's Holiday Spectacular project on the longest night of 2020. I hope *Finding Sanctuary* brings you the same kind of solace and comfort here in 2021 and in the years ahead.

There's an old Appalachian Mountain tradition of celebrating Old Christmas Eve, brought over by the Scots-Irish who settled these mountains years ago. While my immediate family didn't observe either Old Christmas Eve (or Ascension), I grew up hearing about it. So I set out to bring the various meanings of the lovely holiday together into a modern story full of love. The calmer celebration, the animals talking, the January date, and most of all, a different path to paradise, all play a part in *Virginia's Last Old Christmas Eve*.

And finally, the holiday story that's the closest to the mainstream since it's a holiday romance, and even features a cat. But *The Magic Cat of the Hidden Springs Inn and Spa* takes that familiar beginning and bounces off in its own direction. The inn itself takes holiday madness and joy to the next over-the-top level, and the handsome single guy volunteering to work Christmas Eve isn't the typical romance leading man. Neither is the leading man caught in a blizzard and desperate to get home. Add in a very confident, very sassy tabby cat put together out of spare parts, and you have a wonderful setting I've returned to more than once, and intend to again.

I hope you enjoy these unique takes on the winter holidays as much as Jason and I enjoyed writing them. And we both hope these short fiction breaks provide you with a much-needed escape from the hustle and busy-ness that December (or any time of the year) can bring.

No matter how, when, or who you celebrate with, we wish you the happiest of holidays!

❄

Jason:

Ah, the holidays. What a magical time of the year.

Of course along with Glinda the Good Witch, Tinkerbell, or pink unicorns, *magical* also includes The Wicked Witch of the West, balrogs, and various hexes foisted upon the unwary. And let's not forget the Little People: the leprechauns, brownies, pixies, and so on. Beings which might do good or ill depending on their mood, and the recipient's behavior.

You won't find any of these in this collection. There's a touch of magic, sure, but for the most part the holiday magic I like is the magic of joy. Or hope. A promise that the close of one year might mean the opening of a better year ahead.

Kari has already told you about our version of holiday decorations. I'll add that we do keep a few glass balls of the tree-decorating variety, but they hang from the ceiling year round.

I like pretty things. So sue me.

But we *do* have our holiday traditions. For us, those traditions consist of connecting with family, whether blood-relations or chosen. Chilling out together and watching the annual *Christmas Story* marathon. Taking in a holiday romance or two.

And, naturally, gorging our brains on holiday short stories. When we're not writing our own.

Like I said, I prefer holiday stories that end on a

hopeful note. A promise of good things to come. Whether the story is about a crime, family feuds, or trouble in paradise, I want that twinkling Christmas tree light at the end.

Take my first offering in this collection, for example. *Ballerinas and Super Cats* takes us to the last scion of a once-wealthy family, who spends his time in the family manse that no longer belongs to the family. Crime rears its ugly head, but in the end all is resolved and we learn some things about family, and get to see that ol' holiday magic at work.

Sometimes folks have a hard time during the holidays. For some, a loved one won't be there this year, or a career crisis has left the tree a little bare. For others, personal struggles make cheeriness a little more challenging. *The Twelve Steps of Christmas* follows Chuck through a couple of hard days brought on by hard living. But maybe the days ahead won't be quite so hard.

The next story is about one of my favorite topics. Kari and I spent several years in Atlanta, where we discovered a delightfully mixed bag of humanity. Between the southern love for oddballs, and the Atlanta *passion* for them, we found ourselves accepted and accepting among a wonderful group of friends we're still in touch with nearly twenty years later.

For *A True Family Holiday,* I wanted to use that

time of my life to visit with people who aren't enamored of the Christmas season, and who don't let themselves be bound by societal expectations. Found family crops up in a lot of my stories, but this one may be my favorite (so far). I really hope I get to visit the holiday house someday, and meet Edward, Carrie, Lenny, and the rest.

My final story in this collection, *Convenience Store Christmas,* is about another group of Atlanta people who've forged their own family ties. Stuart, Bobby, Susie, and Pete the Cat have graced my pages before, and likely will again. People who've spent enough time in small offices or small retail outlets know that when the right group of coworkers comes together, lasting relationships and wonderful memories can appear out of nowhere, especially when the barbecue is good.

I hope all of you enjoy reading the stories in *Uncommon Holidays* as much as Kari and I enjoyed writing them. That you come to like and respect the people peeking out from these words.

And we both hope that your own holidays, whatever form they may take and whoever you spend them with, end with a big, bright, twinkling holiday light in your heart and a hopeful beginning to the new year.

December 2021

Uncommon Holidays

JASON A. ADAMS

Author of Dirk Knight: The Case of the Rustled Ranch

Ballerinas and
Super Cats

For all those who love at will.

CHAPTER 1

Who needs cops when you have The Amazing Super Cats?

And if Cal didn't hustle his butt on back to the Big House with this ridiculously heavy bag of kibble, his toes might freeze before his arms fell off, and the Super Cats would take their cruel, horrible revenge.

They'd yowl and cry like the nigh-starveling refugees they were, squeezing their guts between his legs and falling to the floor in their fainting weakness.

The evening rated a slow stroll instead of full bustle, though. Wentworth Avenue was dolled up just perfectly for the big Boxing Day celebration at Wentworth House.

He walked through the historic district, past

Wentworth Haberdashery, Wentworth Millinery, Wentworth Carriage Repair.

This last was partly interpretational, partly a working carriage house used to repair the estate's classic vehicles. Cal had spent every free minute he could drag away from directing operations at the big house hanging around the place. And the smithy down the alley where they worked metal black, white, and red.

That reminded him. He needed to do a few more reps on the curling bar with his left arm. His right was getting a little too out of whack from the hammer.

He slowed down by Wentworth Cakes and Ale. They'd locked up early, of course. Everyone would be at the Boxing Day shindig. But he could still catch a whiff of apple pie, peach tart, and candied walnuts sneaking out through the door jamb.

Good thing he walked most of his shopping. The C&A had a siren's song he couldn't resist.

The lovely antique (ish) wrought-iron (looking) streetlamps cast a soft, buttery glow from their triple globes. Through the ribbed and leaded glass (plexi), the clusters of colored LED bulbs stayed dutifully tuned to that warm, olden light.

Later on in the week, they'd be set to a rotating rainbow of color, washing the street in that good ol' holiday cheer for the rest of the Twelve Days.

A light snow had fallen that morning, covering

the little mountain town of Sabre Creek in five inches of gorgeous fluff. A nice warmish snow, too, so all the trees and hedges wore their coats of white like so many frosted mini-wheats.

Or like camouflaged soldiers of the 10th Light Infantry, preparing to scale the Reisa Pass during Operation…

Cal shook his head. No matter what else might change, he'd never stop being a nerd. Which was fine and dandy. He might be Calvin Isaiah Wentworth V, but these days the family patriarch preferred multi-faceted dice, a good comic, and an excellent treatise on military structures of the Gallic Wars to anything as mundane as running the family's namesake textile mills.

Not that any of the Wentworth Mills were in Wentworth hands anymore. Not since CW3 and his penchant for buying dodgy stocks and too much brandy in the years before the crash of '29.

Grandma Irene had to sell just about everything after CW3 lost his mills and gave a double-barrel to a piece of his mind, but she'd found enough help to let her stay in the old house until she passed away just after midnight on New Year's Day, 2000. The old gal was an interesting piece of work, but she'd made it into her third century, and how many people got to say that?

He paused across from the manor's intricate black gates to let one of the jingling horse-drawn

5

sleighs pull in. He crossed the street and took a moment to admire the original hand-hammered wrought-iron ivy and flowers that twined through stout bars, turning this many-hundred-pound barrier into a light and airy piece of fairy-tale beauty.

Admiring the gates also gave the horses a bit more time to pull away. He'd been to the stables, even worked up the guts to give Clyde—a mammoth (what else?) Clydesdale that made him feel like an ant—a sugar cube from his palm.

Cal flexed his fingers, still glad they were all there, and walked toward the brightly lit and freshly painted columns of the manor's grand façade.

His attention split time between watching for the occasional horse apple and drinking in the sight of Wentworth Manor, all dressed up and ready for the evening's forty guests and benefactors.

An oversized frosted cupcake of a Victorian, complete with round tower and cupola, sat behind what should have been a completely out of place antebellum-style entrance. Somehow, the original architect had made it work, and Wentworth Manor had been written up in journals far and wide as one of the earliest fusion-concept domiciles in the Mid-Atlantic region.

Wide, granite steps swept upward in twin, narrowing curves to a broad planked rocking chair platform. Four waist-thick simple Doric columns, all cut and smoothed from the trunk of the same single hoary old Eastern Chestnut. All coated with traditional sparkly limewash expertly applied by Larry Bowdre, an old fart who'd been working the grounds since Grandma Irene still put on her dancing shoes from time to time.

A couple of college kids in black tailcoats and blinding white vests and shirts so starched the cured lime on the columns had competition stood to either side of the twin eight-foot-tall studded oak doors, bowing butlerly as party guests climbed the stairs and wafted inside. The one on the right—Jack? Jake?—broke character long enough to steady a woman with Professional Soccer Mom hair and a truly horrible tracksuit in magenta and velvet who stumbled on the marble threshold stone, which hadn't settled as deeply as the wooden bits around it.

Cal made a mental note to thank the kid for asking PSM to put the selfie-stick away in her duffel-sized sequined purse (magenta) and watch her feet instead.

No grand entryway for Cal, however. He scooted around the side of the big stairs to the service entrance on the left. Nowhere near as large and fancy, but this door opened straight into the kitchen, itself bigger than many apartments Cal had graced, and filled with gleaming swathes of modern stainless steel instead of the period pieces in the rest of the manor.

He stepped inside into the frenetic, highly organized chaos of the annual Boxing Day Blast.

Fifteen men and women wearing whites which matched or contrasted with their skin, with hair of every color natural or bottled, milled around like moths in a high wind, rattling them pots and pans and whipping up a huge mouth-watering venison roast, tureens of bisques and purees, loaves of crusty bread slowly risen over three days.

He might outdo the cats on nigh-starvation.

"Thank *goodness* you're finally here!" Cal saw a curly cascade of fiery red over the top of his kibble bag as throaty mezzo-soprano tones set his belly a-quiver. "You've only got ten minutes to get your Lord of the Manor on."

Hair and voice belonged to Katy Braun, his assistant director and talent manager. And everything else that required real organizational skill. Cal was a great numbers guy and kept the books tidy as a pin, but without Katy he'd have to lock the doors and send everyone home.

Assuming he could find the key, of course.

"Hey, Katy," he said, walking over to drop the cat food by their feeder in the corner. "Yeah, it'll just take me a sec—shit!"

Unlike Madame Soccer Mom, Cal couldn't watch his feet with his arms full of kitty slops. So of course one of the Super Cats had picked the perfect time to play roadblock.

The nasal, scratchy squawk of dudgeon told him Clark the Twenty Pound Chonk had done the honors this time. Kent, his slightly smaller tuxedo twin came meyowling right behind, clearly nigh-starved and wilting from hunger, rubbing greedily against Cal's leg.

"Useless little…" Cal decided to set the bag down by the wall instead. Hard to play Señor Calvin Isaiah Wentworth with his neck in a brace.

"Tsk. Such language, Master Wentworth." Katy smiled, checking her watch. "Dinner's on schedule, and all your *servants* are awaiting your generosity. So go on, git! I'll feed the Dynamic Duo."

"That's Batman and Robin," he called over his shoulder. "Clark Kent doesn't—"

A damp dishrag hit the back of his head, so he decided to wait on the rest of the explanation.

CHAPTER 2

Nine minutes later, Cal hustled down the servant's stairs, far narrower and way more plain-utilitarian than the grand staircase of the great hall.

The butler's uniform fit better this year than last. All the shopping walks had done more good than the C&A could counteract, thank goodness.

He looked down at his wrist to check his cuff-links. Good thing, too.

"Jesus, Clark. Go find a mouse or something."

Super Chonk sprawled along a step about halfway down; feet, tail, and gut hanging over the edge as he licked his whiskers and stared up at this plebian interloper in his domain.

"Get a job, cat." But Cal reached to scrub a head larger than his fist as he continued toward the great hall. Katy should be...

And there she was. Dressed in her black and white maid's uniform to match his own servant garb.

She was scanning the crowd and sneaking peeks at her anachronistic smartwatch, probably wondering just where the hell her boss was.

He stepped up beside her and gently bumped her elbow with his. She saw him and relaxed, but not before giving him her best matronly scowl as she straightened the white bowtie he'd insisted on tying himself. Badly. She'd mastered the loving tie-straighten, and liked to use it in her role as Mrs. Elizabeth Wentworth, nee Stockton, young English bride of CW1.

As if great-great-gramps had ever been that lucky.

In the great hall, three generations of Wentworths, including an incredibly young Grandma Irene, stared disapprovingly at the crowd from their canvas prisons around the upstairs gallery. Electric versions of gas lights lit everything with a not-too-bright ambience, with strategic mini-spots highlighting the portraits, maps, and sketches of the family mill.

Guests milled around, sipping champagne and spiced cider as Ben, their chief interpreter, filled the time with facts about the Wentworths and their manor.

"When Calvin Wentworth the Third tragically

passed away just at the start of the Great Depression, his wife and only heir Irene, who was with child at the time, had no choice but to sell the house and grounds. Selena Holland, matriarch of the Sabre Creek DAR, had a love for the history of Sabre Creek, and agreed to purchase the estate in trust, ensuring Mrs. Wentworth could live out her days in the home, surrounded by all the things familiar and dear to her. In fact, upstairs we'll see Mrs. Wentworth's boudoir and drawing room, restored to their original furnishings and décor of 1875, when the first Mrs. Wentworth—"

A little sugar-coated, but that was all right. Grandma Irene gave up the house, but the terms of the agreement meant she got to die in bed (and the DAR probably hadn't expected she'd outlive 'em all), and her take from the estate's income let her live a comfortable life, and leave a good starting stake to her grandchildren.

No more Wentworth fortune, but Cal hadn't started his adulthood nearly as nigh-starved as Clark and Kent tried to be.

Ms. Holland had an almost religious love of the town's past that put Cal's own historical interest to shame. When Wentworth Manor went on the block in 1930, she'd written letters, sent telegrams, made speeches all across four states, all but begging for funds from her patriotic sisters.

And she'd beaten the bank man to the signing

table with more than enough to purchase the manor house, all contents and outbuildings, plus the five acres enclosed by the original brick wall.

Grandma Irene had liked to complain about being a guest in her own home, but she and Selena had stayed friends over the years. In fact, one of the few non-1875 pieces in her bedroom upstairs was a beautiful clockwork ballerina carved from narwhal ivory and enshrined in a crystal ball on the mantel. Some elder Holland had brought it back from some sea slaughter or other, and presented it to his wife. Who passed it down to Ms. Holland.

Who gave it to her poor widowed friend. Purely for friendship's sake, of course.

Cal had been fighting the museum board on including in the tours the little tidbit that Ms. Holland was a *very* frequent overnight guest of the house, and often traveled abroad with Grandma Irene. The Sister-Betty-Better'n-Yous in town had talked behind their hands, but both women were too well-loved in the town for more than a few tongues to wag.

The tight friendship they shared just might explain the engraving on the bottom of the ballerina globe.

To my fair I., the most wonderful person I have ever known. This pretty dancer will long be dust before your beauty fades in my eyes. S.

Sadly, Ms. Holland had passed away when Cal

was only five and he didn't remember her all that well. His dad, CW4, never said anything, but Cal doubted it had been much of a secret in the family.

Especially since Grandma Irene's clothes went from bright and bouncy to somber and plain after the funeral. And for all her perky, good-natured snark when she had company, Cal remembered seeing her winding the ballerina when she thought she was alone, using a tiny silver key she wore around her neck and never removed.

Watching the timeless dancer twirl and spin while her heart leaked from her eyes.

CHAPTER 3

A squall from upstairs shook Cal from his woolgathering. Some guest had discovered a Super Cat, probably right where he wasn't supposed to be.

Jake—yep, Jake, not Jack—gave the drive a look-over, made sure no stragglers lurked, then he and his partner shut the massive doors. Jake took hold of a hanging velvet rope and gave it a tug, sending a deep brazen bong bonging through the house.

Cal sometimes snuck and yanked the rope after hours, when he was the only one left inside. He *loved* that thing. Had since he was knee high to a grasshopper.

He and Katy went to stand in the middle of the thick pile of the replica Persian rug in the center of the hall. The original, which had more than a little wear and was pretty thin from over a century of assorted feet, Wentworth and non-, was now on display in the Highlands Regional Textile Museum out by the old millworks.

All forty guests came chattering down the grand staircase, half of them with hand on rail and Scarlett O'Hara in their eyes.

Sheesh. Big or not, it was just a staircase. But then, they hadn't grown up pelting up and down the silly thing with their cousins.

Herding the guests along came Jake, his butler partner (and that kid was a last-minute replacement whose name had fallen right out of Cal's head), and a couple of housemaids in outfits matching Katy's —excuse me, Mrs. Wentworth's—own.

Once everyone was spread in a rough arc in front of the staircase, Cal held up his hands for quiet and dredged up his Veddy Propah voice.

"Ladies and Gentlemen. I want you to know how pleased we of the household are that you have taken time from your busy lives to join us here at Wentworth Manor for what my dear Elizabeth and I consider our most important celebration."

The four "servants" stepped forward, and Katy handed each either a folded frock coat, or a vintagey lace shawl.

"On this day, the day after Christmas, Boxing Day, my wife tells me that in the land of her birth, her family's custom was not only to send their servants home with boxes of good cheer to share with their families, but also before the leave-taking, to allow *us* the honor of serving *them*."

Cell phones raised on high and flashes flashed as Jake and the others removed jackets and aprons, donning the long black frock coats and pretty shawls. The men bowed to Cal and Katy, the women curtseyed nicely.

"Now then, it is my pleasure to request your company in the dining hall, where my dear Lizzie the Maid and I, Wentworth the Butler, shall serve you and our loyal staff the finest fare to be had between here and never-gonna-get-there!"

Cal raised his arms as the guests cheered and applauded, then bowed and swept his arm toward the correct door as Jake and his cronies led the way to the gut-buster, clicking the red counter in his hand as each guest passed and watching for stragglers.

"Whew! Almost done," Katy said, wiping a melodramatic wrist across her not-at-all-sweaty forehead. "Come help me slop the hogs, my darling husband?"

Cal could think of a lot better ways to spend time with Katy, but a life of gaming and Management of Historical Family Dwellings hadn't left him with a working asker-outer. One of these days he'd—

"Shit," he said, showing the red plastic click-counter to Katy. "Only thirty-nine. Who the hell is missing?"

"Damn," Katy said, finger bobbing as she counted heads around the sixteen-foot-long mahogany table. Not so easy given the squabble between her own height and the towering candelabras and piles of goodies all along the board.

"No time," Cal said. "You go on in. Draft one of the kitcheneers to help serve. Tell them I came down with a sudden attack of the vapours or whatever, but I should return once my constitution blah-blah. I'll go check the rooms."

Katy nodded, straightened the stupid tie again, and dashed around the corner to the breakfast room's door into the kitchen.

Cal quickly made the downstairs circuit. Didn't take long. Like most big houses of the era, every room opened on each adjacent one, meaning a careful jogger could get his laps in without ever crossing his own path.

Nothing. He should probably check the cameras, but he'd wait on that until he knew for sure Number Forty wasn't in the house anymore. Besides, maybe whoever it was just had to take a leak.

Up the grand staircase, keeping to the right side where the bannister was more sturdy and the stairs didn't squeak as much, a quick duck down the servant and guest wing to check the bedrooms.

No one in there.

"I do beg your pardon," he called in his best LoM boom. "I must insist you join the party below. Everyone wishes to have your opinion of the stuffed quail."

Nothing.

Hm.

He glanced in the Matron's Room, Grandma Irene's restored bedroom.

Nothing disturbed on the big canopied four-poster. All the protective display covers still in place over the dressing table and porcelain wash basin and pitcher. Nothing missing from the —

Wait.

Where the hell was Grandma Irene's ballerina?

Shit! His radio was in his basement office, along with everyone else's. They never kept them on during guest nights.

Shit, shit, shit!

Cal hauled his ass back down the grand stairs, ran to the main doors, and worked the heavy, ratcheting mechanism that scissored inch-wide steel tongues into matching sockets in the top and bottom of the jamb.

Didn't have to worry about the back doors, they were shuttered with decorative-looking but highly functional security gates that would take a blowtorch or large truck to open without the key.

Service entrance also not a problem. Guests were absolutely not allowed anywhere near hot stoves. Certainly not after an evening of free champagne.

So. Back upstairs. Number Forty had to be somewhere, and he knew every stinkin' nook and cranny in this place. Even a few he'd managed to keep secret from the rest of the staff.

Maybe not from old Larry the Handyman, but...

Damn. Who the hell would take an old lady's most prized possession? From her own bedroom? There was stealing, and there was just plain *wrong*.

He crept now, or at least he tried to. His breathing might be a little heavy from running up and down the stairs, shopping walks or not.

He was definitely sweating inside the torture chamber of his period butler's garb.

Bedroom after sitting room, he checked every door not normally locked.

Nothing. Nothing. Noth...

At the end of the family wing, Kent the Smaller Super Cat lay on his belly, whiskers twitching left and right along the crack under the mawster suite's water closet door.

Which was shut.

Which was silly, because the 1875-era WC was *also* behind protective plexiglass, and certainly not available for guest use.

"Hello?" he called, striding down the hall. "Who's in there? I've called the sheriff's office, and—"

The door burst open, shoving Kent out of the way.

The cat fuzzed up twice his normal size—his Super Suit—and streaked in a very un-Super way back toward Grandma's bedroom.

A pile of magenta velvet topped with Professional Soccer Mom hair replaced Kent on the hallway carpet, heading full-tilt for the service stairs in overpriced white walking shoes.

"Hold it right there!" Cal yelled, hoping to stop her before she…

The woman screamed before she made it halfway down, the scream turning into a series of thumps and groans as she finished her downward journey in a clump of flailing arms and legs.

The oversized sequin purse hit the stairs long before its owner hit the industrial green and white tiles in the kitchen below. Fortunately for her, a couple of the kitcheneers had heard the commotion and managed to catch her before her hair dented the vinyl.

Beside the purse sat a crystal ball which had rolled free when PSM dropped the bag. Cal snatched it up, checking for any cracks or other damage. He tugged a tiny silver key from beneath his shirt, wound the ballerina just a little. Just to check.

As the tiny dancer gave a twirl and a spin, Clark the Super Chonk lay right where he'd been when the PSM with the Sticky Fingers had, once again, not been watching her feet.

Silly, wonderful, *Super* Cat, part of a Crime-Fighter Pair Extraordinaire.

"Thank you, buddy," Cal said, rubbing that massive head until Clark's eyes, as green as a certain superhero's bane, closed above a throat full of purr.

CHAPTER 4

The rest of the dinner was a smash. Guests raved about the house, drooled over the food, drank enough of the free champagne that Katy had paid the sleigh drivers extra to make sure no one walked or drove back to their accommodations.

Cal managed to make it in for the last round of farewells as thirty-nine of the guests left through the unbarred main doors.

And as one of the guests left through the kitchen and the service entrance with wrists tucked securely behind her back, passing through a gauntlet of DAR reps, manor staff, and one family scion and his assistant director, all of whom had ritualistic Victorian discipline in their eyes.

She carried no ID in that oversized purse, which besides the ballerina also held several pieces of vintage silverware, an ivory faucet handle from the downstairs washroom, and a couple of Wentworth Manor ballpoints.

Maybe Magpie Molly could be the arch-nemesis of the Super Cats?

Sheriff Duncan, who didn't hold to the old-timey stuff nearly as much as the folks at Wentworth Manor, had come on the double, carrying a nifty little gadget that let him snag a couple of prints right there in the museum office and send them along for processing.

PSM—and Cal needed to stop calling her that, since the Professional Soccer Mom hair had come right off, revealing a head covered with short, bristly spikes—still wouldn't say anything, but the sheriff said a whole lot of museums and houses open for tours all through the area had reported items missing over the past few months.

Be hard to get matching prints at those places after all this time, but maybe they'd get lucky at the most recent sites.

Besides, everyone in the room nearly fainted when Cal explained that the narwhal ivory, fineness of the carving, and the incredibly intricate two-hundred-year-old Swiss clockwork meant the ballerina had last been appraised for the insurance at something well north of ten grand.

Not that north of twenty would buy Grandma Irene's piece of her beloved Selena from him. She'd given everything else to the DAR, but this one thing she'd given to *him*. Given to him and asked him to keep safe after she was gone.

So far, he'd kept it where he thought it belonged. In Grandma Irene's room. But now he figured he better find a better hidey-hole.

Maybe Katy could help with that.

Once everyone was out of the house at last, the kitcheneers cleaning up and loading up, Jake and his actor pals off for their own night of festivities, Cal walked the downstairs circuit.

Hm. He knew she hadn't left.

He found her upstairs, in Grandma Irene's room. The ballerina was still down in Cal's office, locked up tight in the heavy cube of Wentworth Family Safe. Dang thing probably outweighed Clark the Super Chonk, and no one was getting his grandma's dancer out of there without Cal's help.

Katy sat on the dressing table's padded bench, staring up at the empty space on the mantle where the little ballerina should be dancing.

Her heart wasn't leaking out, but he thought he saw some of it behind her eyes, just waiting its chance.

"Hey, Katy. What's up?"

There wasn't enough room on the bench for two, so he hunkered nearby, arms resting on his knees.

"Oh, I was just sitting here thinking about what

you told me. About Mrs. Wentworth and Ms. Holland."

She stopped talking. Apparently now it was his turn. He tried for wise and worldly.

"Uh. Yeah."

Shit.

Katy gave him a peek from the corner of one eye bluer than Etta James after a heavy night of Greek tragedy.

Kent chose that moment to creep up and shove his head under Cal's hand. He absently scratched the furry head, trying to draw something, anything, from his Super Cat.

"Say, uh, Katy? I know we're busy and all tomorrow with the cleanup and year-end books, but maybe...uh...maybe..."

A perfect ginger eyebrow slowly worked its way skyward above that blue eye, and the corner of her mouth that he could see twitched a little.

Shit.

"Maybe...I mean, the Cakes and Ale...you know...uh..."

And that was when his other Super Cat Clark decided to headbutt Cal in the butt, knocking him off balance and forward.

Cal flung his hands out, and of *course* one of them just *had* to land right on Katy's knee!

"Goddammit, Clark, you useless piece of..."

"Why, Mr. Wentworth! How *very* forward of you, sir!"

And Cal lost the rest of his words as Katy's hand came down on top of his.

"And yes, Cal. I'd love to have lunch or dinner at the C&A with you tomorrow."

Well, hell.

Cal managed to get to his feet without too much embarrassment, and Katy allowed him the honor of helping a lady to hers.

She didn't let go of his hand as they walked out of Grandma Irene's and headed toward the grand staircase.

Cal looked back one last time, saw Clark and Kent, the Amazing Super Cats, perched on Grandma Irene's bed, where they *knew* they weren't allowed.

But he'd let it slide. Just this once.

As Katy got the lights with her free hand, Cal could have sworn he heard a distant tinkling melody filling the room behind him.

Where a tiny ballerina danced, joined by two fabulous ladies of a different time.

KARI KILGORE

AUTHOR OF THE WORRY TRAP AND WHAT BREAKS A MAN

PUNGENT JUSTICE

A CHRISTMAS CRIME STORY

For anyone facing the holidays
with more dread than joy

You're not alone

CHAPTER 1

J ennifer did her best to ignore the soft sound of her mother weeping and concentrate on the reason for the tears.

And what she could do about it.

Their townhouse complex looked exactly the same as it had when she was last outside early that morning. Row after row of narrow, two- and three-story houses. Faded yellow garage door on the bottom, then either speckled tan brick or muted dove-gray aluminum siding.

Almost all the units—sorry, houses—had at least one late-Eighties model car or truck parked in the short asphalt driveway, nothing too new or flashy. Either more than two drivers at home, or too much junk shoved into the garage.

Stubby little yards on the side units with a holly bush and a leafless stunted maple tree. A few merry souls had draped those weird nets of Christmas lights over the hollies to try to liven up the place and install the holiday spirit. Even in late December, the ghosts of barbecues and cigarettes past drifted through the blustery cold air, damp and smelling of oncoming snow.

That was it, more or less. It was so flat in this bland suburb of Columbus, Ohio, that as far as Jennifer could see, the entire world was made up of dozens of the exact same townhouses on the exact same street, forever and ever, amen.

Except in front of the unit she'd lived in with her father, mother, and usually annoying little brother. That one looked quite a bit different on this day before Christmas Eve, 1994.

The sharp bits and pieces glittering all over the stubby driveway, for starters. The front passenger side window of an old Chevy conversion van held a remarkable amount of glass when shattered with a brick wrapped in an old white t-shirt covered with red and green stains.

The van's side doors hung open along with the passenger door, with one of the side doors screeching as it swung back and forth in the wind. A few bits of travel junk were scattered in the broken glass. A huge Rand McNally road map book from a couple of years ago lay open and face down, beside a bag of garbage from McDonald's.

For some bizarre reason, the bag had been

ripped open and stomped on. Maybe because the mediocre at best food had already been eaten by the people who bought and paid for it.

Jennifer's mother stood a few steps away from the van, wearing her run-around-at-home blue sweatpants and a puke-green housecoat gripped tight around herself. Her long red hair whipped loose and free around her scrunched up crying face.

Little brother Scotty clung to their mom, still in his thin pajama bottoms and *Jurassic Park* t-shirt, silent and staring at the mess. He might be too young at seven to be as hurt as their mom or as furious as Jennifer, but he knew something bad was happening.

Jennifer wasn't sure if she was glad her father was still at his crappy factory job, the one he'd gotten after a long layoff from his much better job in the coal mines in Illinois. Regular shift since it was Thursday, no matter what time of year it was. He'd be working the week between Christmas and New Year's for the first time ever, too.

That layoff had included the loss of their beloved ranch house (entirely separated from any neighbors and with a real yard on all four sides), and the move to this dreary neighborhood in a lame city in a rotten state.

Right before Jennifer's senior year in high school, now underway hundreds of miles away from her lifelong friends.

If her father had been home, he'd be stomping around and swearing, maybe throwing things if the van wasn't completely empty. The assholes had even taken the tire jack, spare tire, jumper cables, and toolbox.

Jennifer was old enough to know he only acted that way to cover up how upset he really was, and to keep himself from crying like mom where someone might see.

As the oh-so-joyous holiday spirit thrived all around them.

The day all the Christmas gifts and the luggage packed for the long drive back home to Illinois were stolen right out of her family's van. And in broad daylight, no less.

Ho-ho-fucking-ho.

"I just don't understand how nobody *saw* them," her mom said in a rough and shaky voice, probably for the tenth time. "Or heard the glass break. It's not like we live out in the middle of nowhere. Or it's the middle of the night."

"They're probably all inside," Jennifer said. "Never saw or heard a thing."

Or they were in on it, at least a couple of them. She already had an idea who to ask, and who to suspect.

"All the presents," mom said. "All our clothes. Scotty's books and games. I guess it was a good thing this time, Jen. You waiting until the last minute to bring your stuff out."

Jennifer closed her eyes, ordering herself *not* to say the angry things careening around in her mind.

Oh yeah, Mom, this is a great thing, being the only one in the family who didn't get ripped off! I'm so happy to see you crying like that, like I've seen way too many times over the past year. It's great to know some jackasses are running around with what you and dad worked so hard to buy.

Instead, she said, "Did the cops say when they would show up?"

Her mother shook her head, wiping at her eyes and nose with her housecoat sleeve.

"I don't think they're treating it as much of a priority. Not with so many people already on the road for Christmas. I'm sorry, honey. Both of you. I'm so sorry."

This time she covered her face with her hand and cried a lot harder.

Jennifer tried to stay where she was, shaking, furious, wanting to hold onto that until she made some kind of plan to deal with this. Or at least until she found the place to start.

But her mother's sobs along with Scottie's were too much.

She walked over and put her arms around both of them.

She still didn't cry herself, though. Not yet.

She had too much to do for that.

CHAPTER 2

When the police finally did show up—almost two hours after the call—Jennifer wasn't surprised to see her mom had been right. The man and woman dressed in turd-brown uniforms seemed bored and in a hurry to get somewhere else as soon as they showed up. They only asked a couple of questions, barely took any notes in their little flip notebooks.

Jennifer wasn't even sure they bothered writing down their van's license plate number or their phone number.

She clenched her fists so hard her wrists hurt when not one but both of the officers (protect and serve my ass) took the time to scold her mother for having the van packed up and sitting outside like that. Never mind that the townhouse was so small they had half their furniture jammed into the garage.

Or the van's locked doors. Or that the van's lack of widows past the front two seats except for a small tinted back window meant someone couldn't just walk by and see everything.

No. Whoever did this had to have *watched* Jennifer's mother and little brother packing that morning.

Jennifer's flesh crawled when she realized the thieves had probably watched her go out for her early run, trying to keep herself in shape in the winter gap between volleyball and track seasons. She sent up a quick thank you to the weather for making her wear sweatpants and a jacket instead of her normal shorts and t-shirt.

As soon as the cops drove away, Scotty reattached himself to their mother's side.

Apparently he hadn't noticed how red mom's face was, how the muscles along her jaw showed.

"What did Daddy say? About all our stuff and the van?"

Mom stared up at the gray clouds overhead, starting to spit snow.

"What do you *think* he said, Scotty?" she said, her voice rising with each word until she was shouting. "'That's wonderful, we'll go out to dinner to celebrate? Just as soon as I get fired from my job for taking a call at work and running home before my shift is over?' Why do you think I'm *stupid* enough to call him at *work* for something like this?"

Scotty stepped away, staring with his eyes wide and his mouth a little round O. Then he ran sobbing over to Jennifer, hitting so hard that she took two steps back. She hugged him and stroked his curly brown hair, glaring at the empty van instead of her mother.

Yeah, of course. Angry, upset, embarrassed by the way the jerks who were supposed to help had made it sound like it was all her fault. And Scotty could be annoying, no doubt. But Jennifer hated it when either of her parents yelled at her little brother like that.

Mom took a deep breath and blew out winter-time fog.

"That's just perfect. Of course it's going to snow." She stepped forward and slammed the van's doors hard enough to make it shudder, one after the other, as if it had caused itself to get robbed. She turned around, her eyes now red and her face pale. "I'm sorry, Scotty. That wasn't fair. I'm upset, but it wasn't your fault."

She held out her hand. "Come on, let's get out of this wind. I'll make hot chocolate. We'll figure it all out."

Scotty squeezed tight, then ran back to mom. She'd said the magic words for him, no matter the time of year or the weather, and as usual he couldn't resist no matter how upset he was.

Jennifer was tempted herself for a second, then

shook her head. Mom's extra rich hot chocolate and marshmallows with her stomach knotted up like this sounded like a great way to make herself sick on top of everything else. She'd grabbed a heavy hooded sweatshirt to go with her sweatpants on the way out the door this time, so she was warm enough.

Time to get away instead of getting more angry, maybe yelling right back at her mother and scaring Scotty even more.

Time to *do* something.

"I'm going for a walk," she said, and she left without looking back.

CHAPTER 3

Which way to go was a no-brainer, even on a day that was shaping up worse than the day they'd left their house in Illinois behind forever. After a right turn out of the short driveway, Jennifer let her feet lead the way, turning onto one featureless street after another without thinking about it.

She *was* thinking about one of the townhouses a few doors down and to the left of hers. Identical like all the rest, with a Honda several years old parked out front. But right beside it sat a brand new gray two-door Mitsubishi.

The same one Jennifer saw in the high school student parking lot.

Playing back things she'd seen at the town-house, but even more, remembering what she'd seen and heard at school. No one had ever known of

Bonnie Lantz working or doing anything else to earn money. But she stood out like a tail light without a cover from the mostly working-class kids from the neighborhood.

New clothes all the time, too, and shoes and jewelry to match. Light brown hair with perfect (and perfectly maintained) highlights, hair that changed constantly, from sleek straight to curly to caught back with a bunch of glittering butterfly clips. Face carefully made up to match whatever painted-on notion of beauty hit the cover of the grocery store magazines each month.

Jennifer was anything but a fashion hound, and she wouldn't have been even if her family could afford it. Money from her part-time job at the mall bookstore went to shoes and clothes she needed for athletics or for her meager savings for college.

When it came to day-to-day, she couldn't possibly care less as long as her clothes were comfortable. Same with her short red hair and stubborn lack of makeup.

But spending those hours at the mall meant she knew all the trendy looks Bonnie cycled through couldn't possibly be cheap. And Bonnie's parents had typical jobs just like Jennifer's parents, not like people who lived a few miles away in expensive subdivisions and mostly sent their kids to private schools.

At the intersection of Rose Lane and Buckeye

Circle, Jennifer walked up another squat driveway and rang a little round lighted doorbell beside a tan metal door exactly like hers.

Rumors circulated about Bonnie, too, and not very nice ones. She and Cassie, another girl Jennifer's age, were often called thick as thieves, emphasis on the *thieves* part. The word was to keep an eye on your purse or backpack around them, and to watch your actual back even more. No one had ever proven anything, at least not yet.

But Jennifer knew what she knew.

She also knew she needed to keep a goofy grin off her face when the door opened and the one bright spot in this whole miserable exile in Ohio nightmare stood before her.

Katherine Lynda Hayes, Lynda to everyone outside her family upon pain of whatever body part she could reach, stood there blinking in all her nerdy, secretly rebellious glory.

Today she wore her Ordinary Brainy Girl on Vacation identity. That meant glasses with thick black rims, pale face scrubbed clean and shiny chestnut hair pulled back into a ponytail. A pair of faded jeans and a black t-shirt with R.E.M. inside a white box let her fit right in both in their neighborhood and pretty much anywhere around Columbus.

Cute enough, sure, by Jennifer's standards and plenty of people at school. Not strange enough to attract much attention or cause any trouble.

It was Lynda's secret identity Jennifer had fallen hopelessly in love with.

"Tell me you weren't still sleeping," Jennifer said, a little bit of the grin sneaking through. "It's almost noon."

"Even if I *was* sleeping, I'm seventeen and on winter break. No way I'm bouncing out of bed at the ass-crack of dawn like you do, dork. I was reading. Come on in."

At the thought of walking into Lynda's reassuringly normal living room, with her relatively happy parents who'd been born and raised nearby, and the solidly middle-class peace and quiet, and the pretty little Christmas tree that went up the day after Thanksgiving and came down on New Year's Day like clockwork, Jennifer balked.

That had been her family up until a year ago, and she'd thought it was *boring*. Dull routine that she couldn't wait to get away from. A world where everything was predictable and no one had their Christmas gifts and everything else stolen from right in their damn driveway.

"Can you... Do you think you could go for a walk? I need to talk to you."

Lynda scowled for a second, but Jennifer's face probably gave the whole game away. At the sight of the one friend she really cared about in this place— more than cared about if she ever had the courage to admit it—Jennifer's hard shield of anger about the robbery slipped.

More than she wanted it to, even in front of Lynda.

"Yeah, sure. Hang on, let me grab my coat. You don't want to come in at all?"

Jennifer shook her head, pressing her lips tight together to keep them from trembling.

Lynda nodded and darted back inside, leaving the door cracked. She came back out after a minute, yelling that she'd be back later. She'd covered up in a midnight blue jacket with a hood and was still stomping into hiking boots.

"What's wrong?" she said as they set off along another endless street through sameness. "Don't lie and tell me everything's okay, either."

Jennifer shoved her chilled hands deep into her pockets and forced herself to start talking. Before she was finished, a couple of tears had squeezed themselves out anyway. She was pretty sure she brushed them away before Lynda noticed.

"God, that sucks, Jen. What are your parents going to do?"

Jennifer snorted. "Probably not a damn thing. The police don't care, and it's not like we can afford to hire a private investigator or whatever. She'll probably get away with it, like always."

Lynda glanced at her, then nodded.

"That was the first person I thought of, too.

Another haul she and Cassie can sell off and waste on bullshit. Okay then, let me ask you a different question. What are *we* going to do?"

Jennifer resisted the urge to kiss Lynda right then and there on the wide-open subdivision street, just lay a good one on her like she'd been daydreaming about for ages. She settled for a quick one-armed hug.

"I *knew* you'd get it. Think you can borrow the car today? I can't drive the van with the window busted out, and Dad won't be home until five. Doubt I'll be able to get out at all after that."

"Absolutely. Mom and Dad always start early with the holiday cheer on Christmas Eve-Eve when they're both off work, meaning eggnog spiked with bourbon. Nothing too dire, just enough to sit on the couch together and giggle and watch stupid old movies on the VCR all day. Not to get too nasty, but I think they wouldn't mind one bit if I took off for a while so they could get down to it."

Jennifer rolled her eyes. The closer quarters in the townhouse made it *way* too clear when her parents decided to get friendly, no matter how quiet they tried to keep it. She'd hate to be around if they were too tipsy to even try to keep the noise down.

"So I'd be doing them *and* you a favor," she said.

Lynda grabbed her arm, sending a jolt of warmth through Jennifer's chilled middle.

"Yes, please! What are you thinking, trying to find where they hid the stuff?"

"For starters. Ever seen that ugly truck Cassie's older brother drives, with the plastic cover over the bed? I spotted him dropping her off at Bonnie's a couple of weeks ago. No way everything out of our van fit into Bonnie's little car, and Cassie drives that junky old VW Beetle. I'm sure they'd want to get it out of the neighborhood anyway."

Jennifer shrugged, irritated that she'd come to a gaping empty spot in her plan.

"Then...I don't know, I guess we can watch for Bonnie to drive away and follow her. If she can possibly manage to sell off our stuff in time to hit the Christmas Eve sales at the mall tomorrow, she'll damn sure do it. It's probably wherever Cassie lives or not far from it."

They walked for a minute, rounding one of the stub yards between units that was full of different sizes of plastic Santas for some stupid reason.

"Well, we could do that," Lynda said, nodding slowly. "Sit out in my Dad's stinky old sedan and freeze our asses off, hoping that something happens. Try to follow a gray sports car on a gray day like this and hope she doesn't lose us. Or maybe, just maybe, I could go back home, grab my Dad's Boy Scout stuff, and get Cassie's address from there. Then we grab Mom's groovy spacevan instead. It has a better stereo."

Jennifer stopped walking and stared at her brilliant friend. Her even cuter than usual friend with a cold wind flush in her cheeks and a smartass smile.

"I didn't even know Cassie *had* a younger brother. And the address is right there?"

"Yep, along with all the other Boy Scouts he's ever been Scout Leader for. Cassie's *older* brother was the Scout, actually, four or five years ago. Nice guy from what I remember. The things you learn from living in the same old dead-end town your whole life."

This time Jennifer did hug Lynda, a bear hug she was relieved and delighted Lynda returned.

"You're the best, I hope you know that. Come on, we can figure out the rest on the way out there."

CHAPTER 4

Out there turned out to be a long way compared to Jennifer's usual go to school, go to the mall, and go back home routine. Lynda had grabbed a book as big as their Rand McNally for the whole country, but full of gigantic close-up maps of nothing but the Ohio county they lived in.

Lynda said it was something her dad did with the Boy Scouts, but she knew how to use it well enough to show Jennifer.

Outside of their townhouse suburb, outside of town, away from stores or roads with bends in them or anything resembling civilization to Jennifer's eyes. She had family in Illinois who lived way out in the sticks, on huge soybean farms, and one with acres full of noisy sheep.

But she'd only been out there a handful of

times, and months trapped in her in-town rut made it feel like Lynda was driving them along the surface of the moon. Even more so since the silver Chevy Lumina minivan had such a long, wedge-shaped front end and gigantic, slanted windshield. It really did look more like some kind of spacevan transport than an Earth vehicle that should be puttering down a bland Ohio road.

The snow made that even worse, leaving only the darker line of the ruler-straight road cutting through the white jumble of flattened farmland. Lynda promised the minivan had chains in the back, even though she was also sure the roads would be perfectly fine.

The most important things for their vague plan were stowed in the bench seat behind them that smelled of coffee and stale French fries. Lynda had also grabbed her father's Polaroid camera he used for Boy Scout stuff and a few boxes of film. Assuming they could find the stuff and take pictures of it in the wrong place, getting it back to the police should finally get their asses in gear.

The other part—the best part as far as Jennifer was concerned—was two of the oversized pocket-books Lynda sometimes took to school on Fridays, and always brought when the two of them ran around together at night.

Right now, their regular vacation clothes were stuffed inside. Usually the bags held everything they needed to shed their dorky teenager-still-in-high-school personas in ten minutes flat. A quick duck into a convenience store bathroom on the outskirts of Columbus (far enough from home to be safe), and Lynda and Jennifer emerged in head-to-toe black.

Clothes and shoes and nails and hair, and more makeup than either of them wore in a mainstream year in black lips and eyeliner and eye shadow. They'd added black leather bracelets and necklaces as they could afford it, studded with silvery or blood-red accents.

Thus transformed, they strolled Columbus's High Street over by OSU, getting themselves into college dance clubs when no one was paying enough attention to card them or notice their age. Wandering around outside and having every bit as much forbidden fun otherwise.

Because the thrill didn't depend on smoking or drinking or even sneaking around as seventeen-year-olds in an over twenty-one world. The whole point was they felt a thousand miles away from their dull, ordinary selves and lives.

Jennifer hadn't had the chance to do any of that before. She'd barely even heard of such things living far away from St. Louis or any other towns with big colleges. Lynda had been the first to open that door, and to teach Jennifer how to turn her own face into an exotic stranger's.

The first to stir up the shivery thrill of having another girl touch her face and lips, too, and the breathless excitement of changing clothes side by side.

Now they were wearing those same disguises— what they secretly referred to as their true selves— in the strange early twilight of a December snow-fall instead of after dark. The makeup wasn't strictly necessary with the navy-blue ski masks Jennifer had grabbed from her own garage, but she was glad they both wore it anyway. The routine itself helped her turn into someone else, to feel safer. She didn't want to feel like her usual boring self.

Because they were heading toward their chance to bust Bonnie and Cassie, and maybe save some kind of Christmas for Jennifer's family and probably a lot of other families, too.

"We've *got* to be lost," Jennifer said, staring at the mostly blank section of the map in her hands. Only the black of the road they were on and fainter gray lines branching off of it marked the page. "Isn't this too far out to go to our school?"

Lynda shook her head and glanced down at the dashboard. "We're only out about eleven miles. Mom told me she still feels like that when she drives to a new place, like she's in the car forever. Then you get back in no time. We already go to the school on the edge of town, remember? Not much else for another thirty miles. Where else *could* Cassie and her brother go?"

Jennifer looked at the big map again, tracing the lines with a black-tipped nail.

"I haven't seen any roads in ages, but it's supposed to be out here on the left."

"Hang on, hang on," Lynda said. "See the trees over there? I bet that's it."

The same telltale bunch of trees in a vast, otherwise flat field that Jennifer knew from Illinois farm country came up out of the snowy gloom. The sure sign of a house with a windbreak all around it.

All at once, Jennifer's stomach knotted.

"Maybe this isn't such a good idea. There's nothing else *out* here. They'll see us coming for sure. We should go back and just forget about it."

Lynda grabbed her hand, and Jennifer forgot how to breathe.

"Calm down, it's going to be okay. Seriously, who's going to recognize us like this? If someone's home, which they may not be, we just say we got lost. You know how people are. They'll freak out and be so glad we're leaving that it won't matter."

Jennifer let out her breath in a rush when Lynda let go of her hand, then slowed and carefully turned onto the smaller road. It was white with snow, but the tips of the gravels still poked through. Thankfully Lynda misunderstood what had Jennifer so agitated right then.

"Don't worry, the road's fine. Barely a dusting. My parents made sure I drove all over the place last year every time it snowed." She smiled at Jennifer, teeth bright and her lips even more kissable outlined in matte-black lipstick. "Look, no tire tracks in the snow, either. Maybe no one's out here at all."

The cluster of trees was barely a mile off the road, and a white two-story farmhouse stood out in the gloom. Jennifer saw a brown barn, long and flat rather than high like a hay barn. A couple of matching buildings stood off to the side, but nothing that looked like a garage.

"I don't see grain silos or anything that could hold a big combine," Jennifer said. "What do you think they're doing out here?"

"Could be cattle. We'd smell it already if they had pigs. They stink to high heaven."

They both peered at the house and barn as Lynda drove by, and saw no signs of lights or smoke or anyone moving around. The whole place looked deserted. Lynda stopped on the gravel road for a second instead of driving on past. Then she hauled the wheel to the right and drove into the flat area in front of the barn.

"I'm sure no one's here," Lynda said, touching Jennifer's hand again. "You sure about this?"

It was everything Jennifer could do to keep her mind on where they were or why instead of forgetting about the whole crazy scheme and pulling Lynda into her arms.

"We did drive all the way out here. I bet we could hide even this big spacevan behind whatever that wall is. There behind the barn."

Lynda squeezed her hand, then pulled forward slowly toward the wall. It looked like unpainted cinderblocks, stacked about eight feet high. When they got closer, Jennifer realized there were three walls, two about fifteen feet long and a short one across the back. The top was open to the air.

"What *is* that?" she said. "Some kind of storage?"

"I'm not going to say until we get out, but I have a pretty good idea."

She parked behind the long side of the strange structure, on what looked like a wide strip of grass and weeds. When Jennifer opened the door, she jerked back and covered her mouth and nose.

Lynda somehow managed to laugh through the thick, horrible stench, like a thousand dirty diapers but with a sulfurous reek.

"Thought so. It's a dairy barn. This is where they're storing the manure for the winter. I think they call it a dry stack."

Jennifer got out, still covering her nose and mouth, and immediately reached toward the bench seat for the ski masks. At least it would cover her nose.

"So you're telling me even though this whole situation is bullshit, we just stepped out into a fog of cowshit? And it smells like rotten eggs on top of everything else! Could this day *be* any more lame?"

Lynda laughed again, then coughed and covered her own mouth. Her eyes were brilliant red against their outline of black.

"Here, give me one of those before I choke to death! I really wish that wind hadn't died down, huh?"

Jennifer only nodded, yanking her own mask on without worrying about smearing her makeup. If the itchy, thin layer of wool did a thing to block the stink, she couldn't tell.

Inside the dry stack or whatever it was, she saw brown piles against the short wall in back, and three shovels propped against the long wall. She didn't want to imagine how awful the smell would be in there.

The wind had dropped to an occasional gust instead of the steady whine back in town, even though the snow was getting heavier. It felt warmer too, as it so often did once the snow finally quit threatening and started falling. A few despondent *mooos* rang out from the barn.

"I've got to get away from this before I puke," Jennifer said, trying not to laugh herself and breathe in more of the disgusting air. "They wouldn't possibly stash anything in with the cows. Let's check out those other sheds before someone gets home."

Lynda grabbed Jennifer's hand again and they ran to the building closer to the barn, made of the same freshly painted brown wood. Despite her stubborn habit of running every day, even on vacation, Jennifer tried to hide how out of breath she was, both from the stink and from Lynda's warm grip. Her fingers felt cold and lonely when she let go.

Jennifer stood on her tiptoes and peered in through a high window.

"A bunch of tools and farm stuff. I'd bet they use that tractor thing with the scoop on front to deal with the shit."

"Yeah, they can probably switch the scoop out with other stuff," Lynda said. "I've seen those before."

The last shed was more run-down, the same brown paint peeling and cracking, some of the boards warped and twisted away from the frame.

"No window on this one." Jennifer grabbed the dirt-caked lock and shook it, but it held tight. She turned it over and pointed at the shiny clean spot where the key went. "I'd bet the rest of the hasp is clean, too. How are we going to get in there?"

Lynda pushed at one of the boards, and it shifted and groaned. The two of them grinned at each other, then rained blows and kicks all around the shed.

The boards mostly held tight until they met around the back, the side away from the road.

When Jennifer kicked this time, the board jumped from top to bottom with a screeching sound.

"Help me with this one."

Jennifer kicked again, then braced herself on one strong leg and pushed at the bottom with the other. Lynda dug her black fingernails into the edge of the board and pulled. With another screech and a shower of sawdust, the board pulled loose at the top. A few good yanks on it brought the whole thing thumping to the snowy ground.

"Well, that's nice and all," Jennifer said, "but I can't see a damn thing in there."

Lynda grinned and held up one finger. She pulled off her mask, revealing lips just smudged enough to look like they'd been kissed.

"The smell's not so bad now, and I'm burning up. If I learned anything from *growing* up with a Scout Leader dad, it's to always be prepared." She reached into her pocket and held up a green plastic flashlight that fit into her palm. "You do the honors."

Jennifer lifted up her own mask, hoping her face wasn't a horrible streaky mess. She took the light and clicked it on, stepping forward.

"Holy shit," she whispered. "All kinds of stuff. Not farm stuff, either."

Inside was mostly empty with a dirt floor, and

what looked like stacks of old gray lumber toward the front. But near where she stood were piles of clothing and shoes, videocassettes and CDs. A huge wad of multicolored wrapping paper was jammed up against the wall, and boxes with pictures of VCRs, CD players, and radios stacked up beside it. A jumble of suitcases and smaller boxes were thrown to the side.

And right there, right up against the wall where she stood, she recognized her own family's luggage.

Mom had splurged on a big set with brown leather and paisley patterned fabric a few years ago, and everyone used them when they traveled together. Only one was open, with a drift of her brother's bright books and toys beside it.

"There it is," she breathed, her heart pounding in her ears. "All of our stuff. Can we get in there? Get it out?"

Lynda yanked on one board beside the opening and Jennifer tried the other. They bent but showed no signs of breaking loose. Jennifer shifted her grip to the same board with Lynda, and braced one foot against the shed.

Lynda grinned. "Together on one...two...three!"

With an even louder shriek that brought a chorus of answering *mooos* from the barn, the board clattered down on top of the first. A couple more solid yanks opened enough of a passage that they could both shimmy through.

"Look at all this," Jennifer said, turning in a slow circle as Lynda ranged the light over piles of stuff that didn't belong in a broken down old shed on a dairy farm. "What were they going to do, open their own mall?"

"Maybe waiting to return it all the day after Christmas when all the store clerks are too busy and miserable to pay attention. Now, what are *we* going to do?"

Jennifer stared at her family's suitcases, the matching set her Mom had been so thrilled to finally be able to afford. Back when they could afford so many things they never even talked about any more.

Their original plan of taking pictures of anything they found didn't feel like nearly enough. Not with the sound of her mom and Scotty crying still so fresh in her mind.

"I say we steal it back."

Lynda gasped, and her eyes lit up.

"What, all of it?"

Jennifer shook her head as she knelt on the dirt floor and pushed Scotty's books and games back into his suitcase.

"No, just our stuff. I doubt we could figure out where all the rest goes. We might just have to let someone else handle that part. Come on, before they come back or we really do get snowed in."

Lynda picked up one of the brown paisley bags

and shoved it through the gap in the boards without another word.

Just a few minutes later they had everything loaded up in the spacevan with room to spare. They even grabbed what she knew for sure was her Dad's toolbox, along with jumper cables, a tire jack, and a spare tire that were close enough out of a whole bunch of them piled up in a corner.

Jennifer stepped out of the shed and took a deep breath that smelled of fresh snow rather than the horrible stench of the dry stack.

"Now what?"

"Now we take pictures," Lynda said. "Like we planned before. Crap, the camera. I left it in the spacevan."

"No problem, I'll get it."

Her whole body warm with excitement and adrenaline, Jennifer jogged across the yard to the minivan. She barely noticed that their footprints were filled in before she slid the side door open and grabbed the chunky gray camera and two boxes of film.

Then she froze, staring toward the faint glow of headlights slowing on the highway. Close to the gravel road heading right toward the farm.

She ran the fastest fifty yard dash of her life getting back to Lynda.

"Someone's coming," she said between pants. "Almost here."

Lynda pulled the camera from Jennifer's death grip and popped the film inside. Before Jennifer could manage to speak again, Lynda jammed it through the gap in the boards and took several photos. The flash fired over and over again.

She caught each little rectangle as they popped out and handed them to Jennifer.

"Okay, that should be enough. Help me get these boards wedged back up there."

The sound of a racing engine carried in the light wind.

Not the deep rumble of the pickup truck Cassie's brother drove, and not the chittering whine of a Beetle. This was a sports car. Mostly likely the brand-new gray one parked outside Bonnie's town-house every night.

"We'll never make it back out there in time," Lynda said. "We'll have to wait and hope whoever that is goes in the house."

Jennifer shook her head, smiling in the dimming light of the snowstorm really settling in.

"I don't think they'll go in the house. I think that's Bonnie's car. And I think I know what I want to do about it."

CHAPTER 5

By the time the gray Mitsubishi turned in and skidded to a stop beside the shed, Jennifer and Lynda were shaky but ready. They crouched side by side behind the shed, waiting through the solid thunk of doors closing, the excited chatter of Bonnie's and Cassie's voices, then the rattle of the shed door opening.

When a light inside the shed spilled through gaps in the boards and lit up the snow in a cold bluish glow, Jennifer and Lynda trotted as fast as they dared back toward the spacevan behind the dry stack. They stashed the camera, film, and the fully developed photos that did indeed show the stash inside the shed beside the pile of luggage on the bench seat.

Lynda grabbed a tube of Blistex from the console between the seats, squeezed some on the tip of her finger, and rubbed it inside her nose. She wrinkled her nostrils and handed the tube to Jennifer.

"It smells like medicine and kinda burns, but it can't hurt."

Jennifer did the same, blinking back tears and nodding. A weird sharp smell seemed to go right into her skull, and it burned way more than a little bit.

"Okay, good call. Let's do this."

They pulled their masks on, took a deep breath, and went into the dry stack.

Each of them got a shovel and gathered up the biggest load of manure they could manage to carry. Then they walked as fast as they could back toward the still-lit shed.

And the shiny new car waiting beside it.

Jennifer shook her head when she heard music, probably a stolen radio meant to be someone's Christmas present the day after tomorrow. At least it should cover up any noise they made walking on the gravel, though the snow was already doing a good job of that.

When they got closer, she relaxed about noise, even if they had to break one of the car's windows. Two horribly off-key voices shrieking along with the painfully high-pitched torment of Mariah Carey's *Dreamlover* should drown out anything short of a nuclear bomb.

They both rested their shovels on the Mitsubishi's hood and tried the doors.

Just like Jennifer expected, they were open. She wouldn't have locked a vehicle way out here in the middle of nowhere, either.

She and Lynda gently swung the doors open.

Picked up their loaded shovels.

And dropped a nice, fresh, healthy dump of manure damp from the snow right onto the front seats.

Lynda covered her mouth with one hand, and Jennifer was afraid the stench had finally gotten to her.

No, she was trying desperately not to laugh.

Jennifer shook her head, trying her best to scowl through her ski mask, and biting the insides of her cheeks to keep from laughing herself. They carefully pushed the doors closed before they ran back out to the dry stack, now missing a few pounds of cowshit.

The put the shovels exactly where they'd found them, then eased the front doors to the spacevan closed.

Lynda snorted out laughter, and Jennifer leaned close and covered Lynda's mouth with her own hand without thinking.

"No celebrating," she whispered. "Not yet. We have to get out of here first."

Tears were running out of her eyes peeking

through the mask, smearing what was left of her eyeliner, but Lynda nodded.

The light was still on in the shed, but Jennifer knew Bonnie and Cassie could step out at any time. Especially if Mariah had stopped with her...music.

Lynda eased the spacevan forward.

Heart pounding and breathing hard, Jennifer gripped Lynda's shoulder as they rolled in slow motion.

Past the pale cinderblock of the dry stack.

Across the open ground, the wheels mashing down their final footprints.

Alongside the shed, where the gravel would make noise even with the snow.

When Lynda swerved wide to avoid the newly fouled car, a face ringed with bouncy waves of hair popped out of the shed door.

Bonnie, with her new hairdo exactly like Rachel on *Friends*.

Bonnie, who shouted and ran forward just as Lynda hit the gas. A spray of gravels flew out behind her, pinging off the Mitsubishi's front end.

Bonnie and now Cassie beside her, who would never recognize the blue-masked faces cackling laughter as they drove away.

CHAPTER 6

A stack of Polaroid pictures ended up at the police department late that afternoon. Snug inside a plain envelope, with Cassie's address printed on the outside.

After the quickest *ever* change back to their ordinary nerdy high school selves, Jennifer and Lynda made another silent-as-they-could manage dash through the snow. This time after Jennifer retrieved the spare key her dad kept tucked in a little magnetic box inside one of their big van's wheel wells.

His car sat in the short driveway, where all the glass and trash had been earlier. The van's window was covered over with the same plastic they'd used to cover the townhouse's spindly window when it got cold.

Everything they'd stolen back from Bonnie and

Cassie was now tucked back safe and sound inside the van.

Ready for what Jennifer hoped would be a slightly delayed Christmas trip to Illinois after all.

A breathless few seconds after they settled back into Lynda's spacevan, the bright blue lights of two police cruisers passed by. The lights kept spinning away after the cruisers parked outside Bonnie's townhouse, cutting through the heavy fall of a serious snowstorm settling in for the night.

The two of them perched on the spacevan's bench seat so they could hide and spy at the same time, giggling madly.

"I didn't think the cops would show up tonight at all," Jennifer said, wiping at her eyes. "Certainly not before we even got home."

"Want to know what I think? I think Bonnie and Cassie had to call for help when they realized they had to either do that or ride in the shitmobile all the way back here. Then the police matched that up with the address on the envelope. That's what I *hope*, anyway."

Another mad burst of giggles ended when Jennifer realized how close together they'd scooted. Their knees touched, and their shoulders did too.

Then Lynda leaned even closer, and the whole world stopped when their lips met.

All the breath left Jennifer's body in a rush, leaving the void full to bursting with tingling waves of heat and color that radiated and concentrated right between her thighs.

She didn't want to think. She didn't want to move from this spot. She didn't *ever* want to stop touching Lynda as long as she lived.

In fact, she wanted to touch her a *hell* of a lot more.

Lynda leaned back, laughing low in her throat and sexy as anything that ever lived.

"That was everything I ever dreamed about," she whispered. "And then some."

"I think we can do better."

Jennifer leaned in for another kiss just as her mother stepped outside the townhouse door. Her hair was pulled back and she wore a regular winter jacket instead of the thin housecoat, but her eyes were puffy like she'd been crying. Jennifer sat back so hard the spacevan jerked.

Her mother had no idea this awful day was going to have a happy ending after all.

Her father didn't know he had all his tools back, and Scotty would be thrilled to have his books and games before he ever opened a single present.

"I should..." She blew out through her tingling lips, trying to calm herself down. At least for now. "I should make sure they don't call the police again or anything like that."

Lynda brushed her lips across Jennifer's—

setting off another burst of internal fireworks—then sat back with a sigh.

"Much as I want to stay right here with you, I guess you should. You have to *promise* to call and tell me what they do when they see all the stuff back in the van. Promise!"

Jennifer grabbed Lynda's hand, looking into her scrubbed clean beautiful face.

"I will, if you promise me you'll have some free time next week. As soon as we get back from Illinois."

Lynda laughed again and winked.

"Count on it. I'll keep you busy all the way through New Year's Day. Now get in there and let them know Santa Jennifer made it all better."

Jennifer scooted over and slid the door open, letting in a burst of shockingly cold air after the heat between them. She turned back to Lynda.

"They'll get their Christmas after all, but I got the best gift of all. Santa couldn't top this even if he tried."

JASON A. ADAMS

Author of Sunlit Spirits and The Trouble With Vegans

THE TWELVE STEPS OF
CHRISTMAS

To everyone who keeps pushing the daisies down.

CHAPTER 1

December snow is a lovely sight.

Today was the twenty-third. All up and down the parking lot and access road, cars frosted with white sat silent. Naked trees and still-green rhododendrons were outlined and capped with fluffy white. No cars came in or out, and hadn't all day judging from the smooth blanket covering the pavement.

Cardinals chipped and chirped as they chased one another from branch to branch, their scarlet coats bright against a perfect sky, bluer than Smokey's flashers and dotted with puffball clouds. The homey smell of wood fire drifted from the old farmhouse across a bare stubbly field that waited patiently for next year's corn.

Chuck Cantrell stepped out on the porch of Halfway Home, the place he'd been staying for the last couple of months. It had started life as a farm-house, been cut up into boarding rooms for itinerant workers, and now served as the only halfway house for recovering alcoholics and addicts in three counties.

Chuck liked it here. He had some freedom, but also felt safe from himself. His seven housemates came and went, and were okay guys for the most part. In the two months he'd laid his weary head in room three, only one person had gotten himself kicked out for sneaking hootch in his room.

Standing on the whitewashed porch, in front of the whitewashed house with its black shutters, white foam cup of Swiss Miss in hand, Chuck felt ready to brave the day. He loved the cheap stuff, even if he had to drink it quick enough so's the cup wouldn't melt. He sipped carefully, trying not to burn his tongue again, slurping up one of those weird slimy plastic blobs that tried mightily to pass for marshmallows.

Fake marshmallows or not, the cloyingly sweet cocoa passing over lips and gums (look out abdomen, here she comes!) took him straight back to boyhood. Drinking gallons of the stuff while the Mormon Tabernacle Choir belted out dog-whistle pitched Christmas carols on the reel-to-reel player. Him, his folks, and his older brother would sit around on the scratchy, turd-colored burlap couch and armchair, footie-clad feet up on the world's heaviest mock-oak coffee table, and bicker about presents, ham, the correct way to drink cocoa and eggnog.

He missed those days, back when everyone got along and no one had restraining orders.

This Christmas was challenging, though.

Two months out of the rehab center and three months from his last bender, Chuck was finally starting to feel a tiny bit more stable. The ol' brain fog had gradually started to clear, and he could actually remember things. What he needed from the store, what appointments he had that week, where he'd left his phone and his keys.

He'd also started packing on a few muscles. A career spent designing computer networks hadn't exactly given him the body of a Greek god, and half a lifetime chasing the next drunk made him look more like a Laughing Buddha.

Since getting sober, though, he'd been working part time on a construction crew. He barely knew which end of a hammer to swing, so he mostly did the scut work. Hauling lumber, hauling bricks, hauling just about anything. He was a damn good hauler, turned out. The job left him worn out at the end of the day, and he slept early, long, and hard.

Didn't leave much time for thinking, and that was just fine. The inside of his head was a snarled up mess of emotions that he had to *deal* with now, dammit. His days of numbing it all down were hopefully behind him.

He'd be fine.

Today would be a good day, and he was doing fine.

Nothing was going to shake his cool today.

Positive thinking, positive outlook, positive actions.

The army surplus field jacket kept him warm enough, and the day wasn't so cold he had to try and navigate the world in mittens. Good toboggan one of the orderlies at the center liked to knit for all his recovs as he called them.

Warm, full of hot chocolate, good to go.

All well and good.

But this would be his first sober Christmas in… well, in a longish while. Not much worry about trouble with the family, not since the separation papers were all signed and official.

Chuck *maybe* fantasized a little about showing up unannounced and being welcomed home with group hugs all around.

Or *maybe* he could keep working at making sure his head stayed out of his ass and let Mary and the kids have the best day they could. They knew how to get in touch if they'd a mind. He'd mailed cards and a couple of small gifts, bought with his own earned cash.

No big sob stories, no pleading, no whining.

Just a note to say he loved them and hoped they had a great Christmas.

Being an actual rational adult kinda felt good, and kinda sucked at the same time. Not that he had a whole lot of experience on how it *should* feel.

And he didn't have any time to mull it all over. A battered Chevy S-10 pickup truck with a giant eagle decal on the hood came pulling into the Halfway Home parking lot. It might have started out red, but was now mostly dust and scratch colored. With one last wheezy rattle and cough of blue smoke, it came to a stop.

The driver's door opened, and something between a grizzly bear and a small mountain squeezed out, wearing jeans and a black t-shirt that proclaimed in huge neon green letters, "Never Give Up!"

"Hey, Chuck. Ready, buddy?" The voice was surprisingly mild for such an enormous guy.

"Ready and willing, good sir," Chuck replied with a smile and a two-finger salute.

The bear-mountain was Fred S., Chuck's sponsor and pretty much best friend. Fred topped six-three, and went maybe two-sixty on the scale. Tattoos all over bulging forearms and biceps, plus the ponytail that pulled all his hair backward until the top of his head could blind a guy in the right light made him look like someone you really didn't want to notice you on a dark street.

But Fred was sixteen years sober, and had taken Chuck under his wing at the treatment center, when Chuck was still confused and shaking like a leaf in a hurricane. The big man had one of the best hearts Chuck had ever run across.

Ex-Special Forces (he wouldn't say which), ex-gang banger, ex-drunk, ex-druggie, ex-you name it.

Now, Fred worked as a counselor at the treatment center, took shifts as house monitor at Halfway Home, and gave Chuck the rides he needed. He also helped Chuck figure out which thoughts made sense, and when he needed to reconsider some brilliant idea or other.

And he'd taken a chance on Chuck and put him to work on his construction crew. That was something Chuck still didn't understand and would never be able to repay.

Chuck climbed in the truck's passenger door, marveled as Fred somehow greased his way in behind the wheel.

Fred cranked up, gave a satisfied nod at the backfire, and headed out to the main road. This morning's meeting was at the Clubhouse, which didn't look like any clubhouse Chuck had ever seen. It was a storefront in a mostly-empty mini-mall out by Highway 7, about five miles from the Home.

Meetings ran every other hour, swapping out between AA and NA. Chuck sat in on a couple each day. He didn't care which, since he'd never met anyone in the rooms who wouldn't take whatever they could get when they were in a hurt.

They sat in companionable silence for a few minutes. Fred drove with one hand on the wheel and the other resting on the stickshift.

Chuck stared out the window at the clear blue sky with its cottonball clouds, the snow-covered fields, the houses and shops. He picked at his jeans, fingernails flicking at the seams.

"So how you doing, Chuck?" Fred asked, eyes still lazily watching the broken white lines slip past.

"Okay, I guess. I mean, I'm fine." The hand not worrying his jeans drummed on the door's armrest.

"Gimme a better answer, buddy. No copouts."

Damn. Fred didn't like one-word answers when it came to how Chuck was doing.

But he *was* okay.

Fine.

He just…just…

And it spilled out.

"I miss my wife, Fred. Her and the kids. I don't think I'll be seeing them for Christmas and that's eating at me. I want to call her, call *them*, but I don't want to upset the family any more than I already have, and I have no flippin' idea what to do about all of it."

"No shit." Fred glanced over at him and smiled. "Be crazy if you didn't feel that way. What'd ya have for breakfast?"

The sidetrack threw Chuck for a second, but he rallied. This wasn't the first time he had to deal with Fred's train of thought, which sometimes seemed more like a hovercraft than a train. A hovercraft in a high wind.

"Hot chocolate. Couple of cups. I wasn't really hung—"

A loud rumble from the vicinity of his navel outed the lie before he finished.

They both laughed. God, it felt good to laugh. Really laugh.

He'd missed that a lot the last few years.

"Tell ya what, buddy," Fred said, hitting his turn signal as he downshifted. "We'll skip the morning meeting and grab some eggs. My treat."

CHAPTER 2

Chuck sat across from Fred at one of those somehow clean but greasy tables local hash-slinging joints always seemed to have. He told Fred stuff he hadn't even realized he'd been struggling with.

About how he wanted to spend Christmas with Mary and their girls, Sally and Joyce. Sal was heading toward thirteen, and Joyce had just turned ten. He'd already missed a big chunk of their childhoods, too blitzed to pay attention. He wanted to be in their lives, but was afraid they wouldn't ever want anything to do with him again.

He had no idea how to approach any of them, and it was weighing on him.

He hadn't even known all that was on his mind, at least not consciously. He'd been so busy making sure everything was *fine* and *okay* he forgot to check on the things that weren't.

Fred didn't say anything. Just sipped his coffee and nodded from time to time. When Chuck finally wound down, Fred set the mug down, folded his massive arms and leaned on the table, staring at him with that unblinking blue stare that always made Chuck feel peeled open.

Chuck waited.

Fred didn't say anything.

"So, that's about it, I guess," Chuck said. "Sounds stupid I know, but—"

"Shut up," Fred said, expression never changing. "So you feel like you blew it with your wife and kids, and you're having a hard time dealing with the idea of Christmas alone. That about right? A nice summary?"

"Uh, yeah, I guess."

Fred leaned back, grabbed his coffee mug, took a long drink.

"Sucks, don't it? You'll get through it, though. Just keep looking for the next right thing and doing it. Keep your feet on the ground and keep pushing the daisies down instead of up."

Chuck stared at his so-called sponsor.

"That's it, Fred? *That's* your advice? What the hell does that even mean, 'the next right thing'?"

"I dunno, buddy. We all have to look for our own right things. The simple version is TTBFN. Try to be fucking nice." Fred grinned at him again. "Hold doors open. Help little old ladies get stuff down off the top shelf. Don't leave the bathroom a friggin' mess."

"But what about Mary? And the kids?"

"What about them? You can't control that situation. Only thing you *can* control is how *you* act. I'm not giving you advice, but if it was me, I'd let things be on the family front for a little while. Don't tell them how much you've changed, let 'em see it for themselves. Things'll work out, they always do. But you have to be ready in case they don't work out the way you want. Now, let's eat and get our sorry asses to a meeting."

And that was all Fred would say on the subject.

Suddenly, Chuck was starving. His belly had apparently been full of nerves and bile, because once it was all out, he needed food like, well, like someone who hasn't eaten well for days.

Chuck raised a hand to signal the waitress. A hand that held not a trace of the DT boogie.

He plowed through a plate full of scrambled and toast, drank three cups of coffee, and polished off a side of cheese grits before he managed to push himself back. He'd know in a few minutes if the peach cobbler could squeeze in.

Fred drained the last of his umpteenth cup of coal, belched, and gave a quick shake of his head.

"Yeah, forgot to tell ya. The Clubhouse is

getting fumigated this evening, so no meetings tomorrow while the crap settles out of the air. You been doing good, getting at least a couple a day, so you can take tomorrow and just chill at the Home. You'll still get your ninety in ninety, no sweat. So put your feet up on the coffee table. Watch bad TV. Take in a Hallmark movie, maybe."

"You sure?" Chuck asked as Fred dropped bills on the table and they both stood and got their coats. "Need a hand with anything at the job site or anything?"

"Chuck, tomorrow's Christmas Eve. I ain't planning on going anywhere *near* the job, and neither are you. I got some family stuff of my own to take care of. So try and relax a little, would ya? Part of this whole getting sober deal is learning how to do nothing when the time's right. Do nothing, and enjoy it."

CHAPTER 3

They got to the Clubhouse with half an hour to spare before the eleven o'clock. Chuck stood outside with the liar's club, telling stories and laughing some more. They were a great group, pretty even between men and women, but of all ages and social strata.

Jodie, a tall African-American with the shoulders of a boxer and a day job banging the gavel at some courthouse or other, had them rolling with a story about how he threatened to throw a cop in jail. While said cop was arresting him for drunk and disorderly.

Who but a group like this could guffaw over stories that involved so much dumbass thinking? Stories like Jodie's helped Chuck not feel so stupid when it came his time to share in the meeting.

No matter how boneheaded his stories were, someone had him beat.

Of course, they probably thought the same about him. Everyone's road to hell was different, and most people wouldn't trade mistakes.

Since starting this whole recovery jazz, Chuck felt like he truly fit in for the first time in his life.

They went inside, had a good old-fashioned gratitude meeting. Chuck talked about how he was grateful to be sober, grateful to Fred for giving him a chance to work, grateful he'd remember Christmas Day so long as he kept doing what he was doing.

He tried to feel good about the people who spoke of being grateful for the chance to spend the holidays with their families. He *was* happy for them.

But jealous as hell all the same.

The meeting closed out with the usual hand holding and Ah Faddah. Fred made the announcement about the Clubhouse closing at six that evening for the bug sprayers.

"What about Christmas Day?" asked a newcomer woman named Gina, a little nervously. "Will there be meetings on Christmas?"

"You bet," Fred said. "Doors will open at nine in the morning, and we'll keep the coffee on for the duration."

Several people breathed a sigh of relief.

As they left, Chuck looked at the lights decorating the Ace Hardware two doors down.

"Think there'll be much of a crowd on Christmas Day? Won't most people be home with their families?"

"You'd be surprised," Fred said as he unlocked the passenger door. "People need a place to go on holidays even more than other days. Sometimes *because* of their families. But you'll get to see for yourself. I'm gonna need you to open up and stick around until I can get here." He took a shiny brass key from his pocket and handed it to Chuck. "Think you can do that, buddy?"

Chuck stared at the key in his hand. Gulped.

Fred clapped him on the back with a paw the size of a hubcap. "Buck up, pal. All ya gotta do is open the doors and start the sludge pot. I won't even make ya chair any meetings. This time. Hop in, let's get you back to the Home. Don't forget, sock feet and bad TV all day tomorrow. Call me if ya need, don't matter what time."

CHAPTER 4

Chuck sweated through his day of so-called indolence.

He tried. He really did.

Sock feet. Coffee table. The Hallmark Channel.

But his damn brain wouldn't leave him alone.

He was the only one in the Home today. Everyone else had Christmas Eve plans of one sort or another. He tried calling Fred, got voicemail. So he left a somewhat coherent message, and did the only thing he could think of that might get his mind off his mind.

By the time Fred called him back, Halfway Home sparkled from top to bottom. He'd washed windows, swept and mopped all the public floors, scrubbed the kitchen counters down to the bedrock. His arms and back were threatening to go on strike when the phone finally rang.

"Hey, buddy. What's up?"

"Hey, Fred. Just needed to talk to somebody. I've been thinking again."

"Uh-oh. That's always trouble for guys like us."

Chuck heard laughter in the background.

"I don't want to keep you. Go ahead and get back to the family. I'm just doing a little cleaning around the place, and—"

"Don't worry about it. I got time. Talk to me, Chuck."

So he did. Not about anything important, just chatted. It felt good to just chat. Fred already knew what was eating at Chuck, no need to go over all that again.

By the time they said their goodbyes and hung up, he felt better.

Not perfect, not great, but better.

Maybe he'd give Hallmark another chance.

Huh. Turned out he liked several of the movies after all.

CHAPTER 5

Christmas morning dawned bright and clear. The thermometer read right at thirty-two, not bad for December, and the weatherman promised a high close to forty.

Chuck decided he'd walk the five miles to the Clubhouse. If he kept up a good clip he'd stay plenty warm, and the walk would do him good.

He left the Home at seven, and hustled up the road. Hardly any cars were out, and he smiled and waved off the few who offered him a lift. It felt good to be out on the road by his lonesome.

Counting his steps kept the demons at bay, and he made it to eleven thousand four hundred and sixty-eight by the time he slotted the shiny brass key in the Clubhouse's glass door at eight-fifteen.

Gina came in just as the first pot of coffee

finished its noisy drip cycle, and helped him get the readings and pamphlets laid out on the long tables. They were joined by a dozen others by nine o'clock, and the first meeting of Christmas Day got underway.

Chuck was surprised by the soft camaraderie of the group. He'd never noticed before.

Before, he'd been New Guy, too busy worrying about not sounding stupid to pay much attention to everyone else. Things were different today.

Today, the Clubhouse was *his* responsibility.

He knew some of the folks who came in, got to know others. People glad to have a place to go on Christmas Day, glad to have others to share the day with.

Over the next few hours, he brewed dozens of pots of coffee, both hi-test and decaf. He chaired a couple of meetings, sat and listened at a couple more. People came and people went, but he didn't think he saw less than ten folks at any given time. Chuck shared his story, shot the shit between meetings, introduced himself time and time again.

It struck him around three when they sat down to several steaming pizzas, loudly blessing the local Dominos and tipping the delivery girl handsomely, that he was having a good day.

No, better than good.

Chuck felt great, actually. He was truly enjoying

himself, and hadn't thought about Mary and the girls more than a couple of times all day.

Part of it was staying busy, of course, but part of it was the sense of belonging. Of helping out by helping others. Yeah, he wasn't changing the world or saving lives, but he was here, making sure the doors stayed open and the coffee stayed fresh.

He was sharing what little experience, strength, and hope he had, and got to soak some in from all the others.

The last slice of cheese pizza sat lonely in the last box, while a bunch of ex-drunks too polite to do more than stare greedily instead of dueling to the death tried to ignore it. The bell over the door chimed, and Chuck stood and turned, ready to welcome the latest addition to the day's festivities.

And stopped dead.

Mary came in, followed by Fred.

Chuck couldn't do more than try to winch his jaw back up. He wanted to say something. Anything. But there was some sort of major disconnect in his brain wiring right then.

"Hey buddy. Told ya I'd make it," Fred said, grinning like a cat in a canary-processing plant.

Chuck goggled his gaze between Fred and Mary. She looked so damn good in her poofy blue winter coat, the one with the fake fur hood. Her cheeks had that rosy blush she always got when the temperature went south of sixty. Her ebony curls had that tousled look they only got when she'd had her hood up.

"Hello Chuck," she said. She wasn't smiling, but she wasn't frowning either.

"H...Hi, Mary. How are you?" Eloquent as always, but at least he got some kind of words out.

"I'm fine. You look better."

Chuck choked on a laugh. God he wanted to take her in his arms.

Instead, he shoved his hands in his pockets. Gave her a smile.

"Yeah, well. That's a pretty low bar, considering." This time she laughed.

"How did you... What brings you out here, Mar? It's great to see you, but I wasn't expecting to."

"Blame Fred," she said. "He called me, told me I might want to come see how you're doing. We... we talked. Quite a bit."

Chuck shot a glare at Fred. "How the hell did you know Mary's number?"

Fred gave him that goddamn grin of his.

"Ya gotta quit leaving your phone laying around, buddy. Oh, and there's this great new feature phones have, where you can make it so you need a code to unlock it. You might want to look into that."

Chuck felt his eyes rolling. "What happed to rigorous honesty, oh sponsor-mine?"

"Hey, did I tell you I *didn't* sneak and check your contacts?"

He pondered the possibility of taking Fred out. Wondered what sorts of power tools would do the trick.

"We've been outside for a while, Chuck," Mary said. "I've been watching you. Watching how you've been taking care of people in here."

"Not really. I just make the coffee and straighten up in between meetings."

"No, you do more than that. You've been talking with people. And it looks like you've been listening, too. I think this suits you, and you certainly seem calmer and happier than I've seen you in a long, long time."

He didn't have an answer for that. Just looked at his feet. Kicked the carpet with one toe.

"Sally and Joyce miss you, you know."

"I…" he had to swallow. Swallow hard. "I miss them too, Mary. And I miss you. I'm really, really sorr—"

"Don't," she said, raising a hand. "Not right now, okay? I'm not making any promises, and I don't want you to either. But I think it would be good for the girls if you want to come by later on this evening and tell them Merry Christmas. They're at my mother's now, but maybe around seven? You can hang out for an hour or so. Yeah, an hour would be good, for now."

Chuck didn't know what to say. He looked at Fred, who only shrugged.

"Your call, buddy. I said you had to stay until I got here, and I'm here."

He looked back at Mary. Saw her looking back at him.

Not with welcoming desire, not by a long shot, but still.

She had just offered him a Christmas gift bigger than any he had a right to.

"I'd love that. Thank you. Thank you so much, Mary. Look, you go on back to your mom and the girls. I'll…I'll text you when I'm on the way."

She put her hand on his arm. Just for a second, then she drew back. Turned to leave.

"Call me when you're on the way, okay? I'll let the girls know you're coming."

Chuck's eyes burned as he watched her walk out to her little Corolla. Car could use a good wash and wax. Get the salt off.

Maybe she'd let him do that for her.

He felt Fred's heavy arm fall across his shoulders.

"Good woman there, buddy. Don't blow it. One hour's all you get today, but it's a start."

"Can…can you maybe give me a ride over?"

"Sure thing, buddy. Not a problem. And Chuck?"

"Yeah, Fred?"

"Merry Christmas, you old smoothie, you."

And Chuck felt more of that glorious, wonderful laughter bubble up and out.

KARI KILGORE

AUTHOR OF THE WORRY TRAP AND AT THE HEART OF IT ALL

FINDING SANCTUARY

A STORY OF LONGEST NIGHT

May you find a bright spot in the darkness
of your Longest Night

CHAPTER 1

J une had never actually said it out loud to anyone, but Longest Night had become her favorite service at The Sanctuary. No matter if the crowd was large or small, the weather unseasonably kind or typical Midwest brutal. She looked forward to this special, sacred time with the people she ministered to more than any other holiday.

Tonight the crystal-clear southern Illinois skies cooperated, along with the wind chill, and she stood outside with only a charcoal-gray hoodie with the hood up. More than enough protection for her, with the drifting aroma of wood smoke livening up the otherwise still air. Most folks walking toward the octagonal stained glass delight of their converted Seventies church were bundled up a good bit more, with temperatures falling below forty after the sun went down.

When they asked if she wasn't *freezing*, June smiled and shook their hands with her own warm from her pockets or gave them a big, cozy hug. To younger people or to men, she usually just said she'd grown up farther north in Michigan, so she was built extra tough. That much was true.

But with ovary-equipped people around her own age of fifty-one or older, she could be completely honest.

June had proudly reached the biological stage of life where the meaning of hot and cold changed dramatically. Pre-hot flash so far, but far more likely to turn the heat down rather than up when she was home by herself (which was *all* the time now). And thankful every single day that the miserable, humid summer in her adopted hometown of Laconia was a long way off.

Under the hoodie, she wore her usual Longest Night dark green dress with jewelry in sparkling red, including strands twisted through her braided chestnut-streaked-with-silver hair. Colors that said Christmas to many, and that was fine with her. Quite a few members of The Sanctuary's secular congregation celebrated Christmas with joy and enthusiasm.

The red and green combination said renewal to others who tended toward pagan beliefs. Many of them would be gathering in a generous farmer's field later on to celebrate with a spectacular solstice bonfire and ceremonies of their own. She normally loved the bonfire, but doubted she'd be up for a big celebration this year.

Tonight in The Sanctuary, the idea of renewal held even more meaning. June always picked the astronomical winter solstice for holding Longest Night. Acknowledging the idea that the sun would now begin a long, slow return made sense, but this service was about so much more.

June wanted to help those in need—in mourning or in pain or seeking comfort for whatever reason—and let them know renewal of life itself would someday bring warmth just like the returning sun. The promise of spring, no matter what held people in the depths of emotional winter.

The two huge rectangular parking lots shone under the nearly full moon, with nowhere near as many cars as they had for other special services or even the usual Wednesday nights and Sunday after-noons. She'd only started observing Longest Night seven years ago, but everyone in the congregation, in Laconia, and in other towns nearby knew about it. They'd likely welcome people from all denomi-nations tonight, along with folks who hadn't attended any sort of religious service for years.

Not having all that many people who felt drawn to mark some significant passage in their lives was a good thing. And June loved the intimacy of the smaller gathering with such a challenging topic.

She already knew the stories of many of the people she greeted as they walked inside. Either directly from them in counseling or recovery meetings, or from the gossip that flew around a secular congregation every bit as much as a religious one.

Lost mothers or fathers, sisters or brothers, spouses or partners. In mercifully few cases, lost children. Lost pets that cut almost as deep, deeper for some. Friends lost through death or simply falling out of touch. Tough medical diagnoses. Job changes, kids leaving home, retirement. All manner of life changes, big and small.

And oh, so many breakups.

June was always grateful to be there for her congregation through all those life struggles and transitions, and to help them be there for each other. She'd openly changed along with them through her own transitions and losses and often spoke about them during the service.

This year, the major change in her life felt like long ago, in the endless gray days between the New Year and Valentine's Day. When the fraying ties between her and Les had finally parted. A change she'd kept mostly to herself, even though everyone knew as soon as Les disappeared from all their lives.

June's original reason for not going with the

traditional name for this service, Blue Christmas, had never felt so valid as on this night. She never wanted to spoil her lifelong love of Elvis by hearing that song in her head all night long. Especially when the lyrics perfectly described how she'd felt during her first long, awful weeks alone.

Whether she spoke about it or not, Longest Night felt like the perfect time to put all of that behind her and find the way to whatever came next.

CHAPTER 2

The chilly air bit into Ryan's nose and ears as soon as he stepped out of the car. He glanced up at the bone-white moon overhead without a cloud anywhere nearby, and reminded himself to be glad it wasn't much colder, raining, or snowing.

He zipped up the absurdly oversized winter jacket he'd borrowed from his father as he hurried around the car to help his sister. Only a few busy days back in Illinois hadn't given him enough time to go shopping for one that actually fit him, and hopefully one manufactured later than the mid-Eighties. He had to admit the poofy sky blue monstrosity was nice and warm.

A rich childhood memory flashed up when he caught the wonderful scent of a wood fire not too far away. His dad in this coat, himself in one smaller but no less embarrassingly Eighties, a bunch of Boy Scout buddies in a similar getup. All of them roasting marshmallows, trying hard to catch theirs on fire long enough to be melted but not inedible.

Gods, when had he last roasted a marshmallow? He could do with about a dozen of them right now, gooey and sweet and sticky hot.

Erin already had the door open when he got there, and she took Ryan's offered arm without protest. He tried to avoid the memories about her, especially the ones that made it painfully clear how difficult the years had been for her. But faded snap-shots from their childhoods washed over him anyway.

Instead of the strong and healthy girl or young woman with a defiant attitude—and a soft spot for her big brother—the Erin who pushed herself up out of the car looked fifteen years older than he was at forty-eight. Curly brown hair thin and graying far more than his, face lined with more wrinkles than their father had. Her grip on his arm was getting stronger, but her hand was still so painfully thin.

All the years she'd spent lost in an alcohol- and drug-induced haze had etched themselves into her body, along with the abuse she'd suffered from a so-called lover right before she finally got herself free.

Her mind, though, her hilarious and smartass bratty little sister mind? That part was recovering nicely. Her eyes sparkled more than he'd seen in a long time, and she laughed more than she cried or yelled.

She'd seemed quiet and melancholy all day, but Ryan was pleased she'd wanted to come to this new Longest Night thing even if he didn't understand why.

They walked toward the old church neither of them had been to since they were bratty pre-teens. Their parents had been casual Methodists, but parking the kids at the friendly First Christian Church for Vacation Bible School made all kinds of sense. Ryan had fond memories of laughter and crafts and goofy puppet shows with good life lessons.

What he saw by the moonlight was a huge octagon made of brick, peaked in the middle but without the curvy old Seventies-style cross. Each wall held a beautiful stained glass window, the angular impressionistic shapes glowing with inner light, as did the high center of the roof. He had to admit it looked more welcoming than he'd expected after so many years away.

"At least no one will know me here," Erin said.

"Care to translate that one, kid?"

"No one I have to apologize to. Make amends to. I can just be my gloriously fucked up self."

Ryan rolled his eyes and they kept walking. He'd picked up right away that talking about how messed up she was helped Erin cope somehow. He suspected she liked the control of saying it herself before someone else could point it out to her.

Enough people had pointed it out to her to last a lifetime.

He and people who understood what she'd been going through—and Erin when she was in a good state of mind—knew very well how much progress she'd made, how dramatically *less* of a hot mess she really was after weeks in rehab and a couple of months in a halfway house.

Ryan was so proud of her he could burst. And he knew he needed to keep that to himself when she was in a mood like this.

"We'll be a matched and messed-up set," he said. "We *both* just moved back into our Dad's house, and I haven't set foot in anything resembling a church for longer than I can remember. I think we'll both be okay here, especially tonight."

A woman stood in front of a set of huge double doors inset with more stained glass, shaking hands with or hugging everyone who passed by. She wore a gray hoodie so exceedingly ordinary that Ryan was a bit envious, not to mention self-conscious about his vintage winter garb.

But her face and her smile in the glow of all that beautiful glass was a million miles from ordinary. She had high cheekbones and a deep cleft in her chin, and even from a few yards away he saw the way she looked into every person's eyes. This was no routine meet-and-greet or some kind of shove-everyone-through receiving line.

This woman took the time to connect with every person who came into her orbit. He did his best to tamp down his brain's predictable, irritating question. How long since *he'd* connected with someone like that? Or since he'd let anyone connect with him?

Erin displayed another sign of how much she'd recovered when she read his mind effortlessly, like she had when they were those bratty kids.

"See something you like, Ry? Is she why you were so eager to come with me tonight?"

He snorted and shook his head. "I wouldn't say I was eager. You might recall this started out as Dad's idea, smartass, because it helped him when Mom passed away. Anyway, I think I'm getting too old for love at first sight or some other such nonsense."

Erin laughed out loud, the high, delicate sound sharp and clear in the quiet night. And the most wonderful music to Ryan's ears.

"Oh yeah, positively ancient. I'm not the only one who needs a new direction, brother. A new focus."

Ryan resolved to keep the witty comebacks he wasn't coming up with to himself. Erin had a point. His divorce had gone through more than two years ago, but he'd lingered in her native Florida anyway.

Not out of some pitiful hope that his ex would come to her senses and want him back again. More out of some strange nostalgic wish that his life wouldn't have to change all that much after all.

Even though every single thing had changed.

When he'd gotten the offer to work remotely within a few days of hearing Erin would move back to Laconia, Ryan finally accepted his own altered reality. After decades away, home and family and a change he made for himself made all kinds of sense. Their father and the rambling white house with black shutters had welcomed both of them home without hesitation, and blissfully few questions.

He tried to play it cool, but his attention and gaze kept returning to the woman greeting everyone. Reverend June Fitzsimmons, he assumed from his brief peek at the website for The Sanctuary and Longest Night. The same smile from her online photo never looked fake or forced, but sometimes she greeted people with a somber expression that made his heart ache.

He had no doubt she knew these people inside and out, and cared deeply about all of them. Even the ones she'd only met that very moment.

What a rarity in all too much of his world.

Before he figured out what to say or how to get ready to meet someone he was indeed attracted to at first sight, he and Erin stood in front of her.

"Welcome to Longest Night," she said in a smooth, deep voice. "I'm June."

Her smile warmed his heart and every other shivering part of him, and thank all the powers that be, her hand warmed his freezing one.

"Good to meet you, June," he managed without incident. "I'm Ryan, and this is my kid sister Erin."

June studied Erin for a second, then pulled her in for a hug. Erin gasped, but after a second she squeezed tight. Ryan tried not to wish June had hugged him, too. June looked back at Ryan then, and something in her eyes had his belly turning silly little-boy flips inside.

That smile…

"I'm glad you're both here," she said. "I'll see you inside."

CHAPTER 3

J une lingered outside for a few seconds when no one else was pulling into the parking lot or walking toward her, and only a few minutes remained before the service started. This was another advantage of cold weather that she was grateful for.

On balmy afternoons and evenings, people often lingered with her until she led them all inside. She sometimes stole a few moments to herself as they got settled, sure. But this—enjoying the quiet of the night, breathing in the cold air, turning her face toward the moonlight—helped settle her like nothing else could.

She surely needed a bit of settling. June smiled, glad all over again that no one could see her.

Why had Ryan affected her so? She'd never seen him before, and a few words and a brief handshake was what she did with anyone who walked through the doors of The Sanctuary. But she couldn't seem to shake the angles and planes of his face, the silver glinting in his reddish beard, the warmth of his eyes and smile by the light of the moon and the stained glass behind her.

And while his hand had been freezing cold, the spark that flared up in her middle with his touch certainly had not.

June shivered, reminding herself to focus on what people needed tonight. Going by the way he held his sister's arm and the protective way he watched her, Ryan wouldn't have room for anyone else in his mind anyway.

She stepped inside, hanging her hoodie on one of the few empty hooks left in the entryway and pretending she didn't notice the goofy oversized blue thing he'd been wearing. Refusing to lean forward and see if it smelled half as good as his smile looked. She probably wouldn't have been able to pick his scent out in the jumble of wool and sweat and perfume and general human that lingered in the little vestibule.

This room wasn't much. Just a rectangular wooden box for leaving coats and boots and umbrellas and such. Except for those wonderful front doors and a matching pair at the other end, nothing remarkable at all.

The real beauty and magic hit as soon as June stepped into the sanctuary.

She'd made a habit of trying to see the room as the new people might on Longest Night. The way she'd seen it when she first walked inside eleven years ago.

The most striking feature, the one that had sold her immediately all those years ago, was the circular arrangement. The gleaming wooden pews weren't in straight lines with an elevated pulpit in front, or angled toward a raised stage. They sat in rings around a slightly lower area in the middle, with burgundy carpeted aisles between like spokes on a wheel.

Another carpeted circle waited in the middle, large enough for June to take several of her long steps across. She kept a simple wooden chair there, and a table big enough to hold paper, books, and a glass of water. Maybe a vase filled with fresh flowers.

When she spoke with her congregation, June paced. Around her smaller circle, or sometimes back and forth. Making eye contact as much as she could with as many people as she could. The only time she sat was during quiet time or meditation.

Pacing also let her see the glorious windows all around them. When the sun beat out, a ring of smaller windows overhead shone down multicolored light. Tonight huge yellow pillar candles were lit between the windows, adding their cozy glow and subtle beeswax scent.

Opposite the doors from the vestibule, a set of plain wooden doors stood open. Inside was a small hot tub the former congregation had used for baptisms when they couldn't go outdoors. June hadn't baptized anyone and didn't plan to, but several tea light candles, matches, and tiny floats were standing by tonight.

June often wondered what kinds of services were held here back in the Seventies when the First Christian Church of Laconia was built. She couldn't imagine a space more perfect for The Sanctuary they'd all built together.

When she got to the center and took her customary look around, her heart absurdly skipped a beat when she spotted Ryan and his sister in the second row. Without the silly coat, he was even nicer looking. A midnight blue button-up shirt fit a heck of a lot better over strong shoulders. His brown hair could use a bit of a trim, or maybe he liked it curling free and touchable around his ears like that.

Sheesh, get a grip, June...

A deep breath, closed eyes, and she was ready.

"Thank you all for making your way here for Longest Night. Sometimes it can be hard to reach out at times like this. When you're blue, or griev-ing, or simply weary. Whatever your reason or what you need tonight, everyone in this room is welcome."

She walked slowly in a circle as she talked, looking at each person in turn. Some gazed steadily back, maybe with red eyes or wiping away tears. Some sat with their eyes closed or stared into space. A few looked at their feet or covered their eyes.

"I'm here to offer comfort, but this isn't a night for the kind of sermon you may be used to, or even one of the discussions we normally have here. If you have a question or something you need to hear me say, please don't hesitate to ask. What we offer tonight is a chance for you to do what *you* need. Tell your story. Sit silently. Cry. Pray in your own way. No one will judge you here. No one."

When she focused on Ryan's sister, Erin only looked back, eyes clear and steady. Ryan seemed to be concentrating intently until he caught June's gaze. Then he smiled bright as the moonlight outside.

June smiled back and kept walking, pretending her heart didn't flutter again.

"Last year we had small groups who talked together, sharing what they needed to and helping each other. I have several books here with passages marked if you'd like to read to yourselves or to each other, or if you'd like me to read a bit. And a few years ago, we started a tradition of lighting candles for those who want to. Then floating the candles in water, bringing our tears and the light of hope together."

She held up the rough, irregularly shaped paper from her table.

"For those who wish, we have a small fire pit out back, and one of the art classes at the college donated this recycled paper they make. Write what you want to let go of, what you want to hold on to. What you want more of, or less of. What you want to forgive in yourself or someone else. A few people always head out to the solstice bonfire later if you'd like to go along and feed a much bigger fire."

June turned in a slow circle.

"All this to say, Longest Night is for *you*. All of you. You're free to stay as long as you want, and you're free to go when you're ready. I know the idea of a light at the end of the tunnel may make you feel like it's yet another oncoming train. The truth is you can all get through. We can all get through, together."

She held one hand over her heart and lowered her head. Then June looked up to see what her newly formed congregation wanted and needed on this night.

As they more and more often did, they were ready to take care of themselves.

Several walked straight to the table beside her, picking up a book or sheets of paper. A few headed to the baptismal hot tub, and the tang of struck matches floated through the air. Almost everyone shifted or moved in some way, closer together or further apart.

As for handsome Ryan—who'd never looked away or seemed distracted the whole time June spoke—he sat in a shoulder-to-shoulder huddle with his sister, whispering back and forth. Erin had the look of fragile new health that would only keep getting stronger if she was ready to let it. June recognized it from the recovery meetings at The Sanctuary.

Discussion concluded, Erin and Ryan both stood and headed straight toward June. Erin moved slowly, but she looked determined. Ryan had a bit of a deer-in-the-headlights stare to go along with flushed cheeks.

"Do you have…" Erin started, then she plucked a secular recovery book from the table, along with several sheets of the recycled paper and as many pens. A few people from the meetings lingered nearby, too shy to come forward but paying close attention. "That's what I wanted. Thank you for doing this, June."

"I'm glad we could be here," June said. "Just let me know if I can do anything to help."

Erin grinned, and June got a bittersweet glimpse of the lively young girl she'd once been. And the healthy woman she could become.

"Just the one thing," Erin said with a mischievous smile. Then she turned and carefully walked away. The small lingering group followed, moving to meet her at one of the pews away from everyone else.

June turned to Ryan with her eyebrows raised, curiosity in her mind, and a whisper of hope in her heart.

CHAPTER 4

Ryan tried to hang back as his entirely wicked and truly evil sister walked away, leaving him standing alone with Reverend June. Erin even walked better than she had since he'd gotten home, slowly but with hardly a trace of the unstable gait of wasted muscles, an injured back, and healing broken bones.

He blinked back tears as several people sat around her. Watching her, looking to her. Maybe recognizing something they had in common that he couldn't quite understand.

Ready to hear to what she had to say. Probably ready to listen, more than he had been when Erin pretty much *scolded* him into talking to June.

Who waited politely, probably wondering why this dorky stranger just stood there.

"She's really doing well," he said. "I'm proud of her."

"It's tough for a lot of people. Admitting they need help. Even if that's nothing more than someone to listen to them."

He shook his head, still watching his sister. "She asked for help by getting away from that...out of a bad situation. Changing her whole life, even moving back home. I don't quite understand why she wanted to come down here tonight, but I'm glad she did."

He finally turned back to see June with a half smile and a merry crinkle at the edges of her big hazel eyes. She was even more lovely indoors with light sparkling off the red stones tucked into her hair, but he wondered how her hair would look in the moonlight, or maybe by that big bonfire she'd mentioned.

Then Ryan played back his own words and smiled himself.

"Is it more obvious that I'm the one who wants someone to listen," he said, "or that I just moved back home?"

"Either way, I'm glad you're here," June said with an adorable blush. "Have you asked her why she wanted to come for Longest Night?"

"It was our father's idea. He said it really helped him after our mother passed away about four years ago. Tom Chambers. Just imagine me taller with all gray hair."

"I'm sorry to hear about your mother. I'm afraid I don't remember your father, but I'm glad being here helped him. Sometimes I think the building itself does all the work."

June's fond smile as she looked around the room sent warm little tingles through Ryan's middle. He was torn between wanting to keep talking to the most interesting person he'd met in ages and wanting to play it cool. Keep himself from getting out there again, maybe getting hurt.

A glance at Erin holding hands with two of the people she'd just met tipped him over.

"I think it's more than the building," he said before he lost his courage. "But I remember how cool the light is when the sun's out. Especially through those top windows."

Now June's eyes lit up, brighter and more beautiful than the stained glass.

"You were here before? When it was a church? What were the services like?"

"I was just a kid, not even in middle school yet. We came to Vacation Bible School here. Puppet shows and everything. I've never forgotten the minister wearing blue jeans and tie dye."

June covered her mouth and held back a giggle that Ryan barely managed not to echo.

She glanced around the room again, and walked toward one of the front pews. Ryan realized as he sat beside her that she'd picked a spot where she could see each of the small groups.

They were all taking care of themselves and of each other. Talking quietly. Holding hands together like Erin still was. Bent over writing or drawing. Staring into one of the big candles. A few crying in silence: sitting by themselves, but not alone.

June let them do what they needed to while she watched over them.

"I *knew* it," she said, grinning. "With the shape of the room and the hot tub and all, this had to be the grooviest church in town. Tell me more, and please tell me you have pictures."

"I'm sure Dad has incriminating evidence somewhere. Our whole generation may have avoided our parents posting mortifying videos online, but bell-bottoms and bad hair are always lurking. Is this all right? I don't want to keep you from helping someone."

She tilted her head with that amused half-smile, and Ryan laughed under his breath, rubbing the back of his head. Well, he did want to talk to June, very much so.

But right now, he wanted to find out everything about her.

"Yeah, okay, I'm finally catching on. I'm at least going to turn the tables on you a little. We know I'm from here, and Dad has the bad photos to prove it. Where did *you* grow up, June? What brought you to Laconia? If you weren't our fearless leader for the evening, what would *you* want to talk about on Longest Night?"

CHAPTER 5

June surprised herself almost as much as Ryan had with the questions and the focus on her. Instead of deferring, turning everything back to him as she so did during services (and lunches with friends, conversations with family, and most of every other time), she talked.

She told him about leaving Michigan not long before her family did with the downturn in the automobile industry there. Studying English, then psychology, and years spent on the West Coast, selling her soul in Corporate America and volunteering at local counseling centers.

Turning forty, selling her house for a crazy profit months before the Great Recession, and driving east with no destination and no plan. Stopping for a long stay to help a cousin in Laconia and falling in love with the little farming town. The rhythms of the seasons that she'd missed in sunny California. The quiet routines of the land and working with it, and the attention and discipline the often-harsh weather demanded.

Ryan never checked his watch or phone, never looked glassy-eyed or checked out. He peeked over at his sister now and then, the same way June checked on everyone else when she paused for a breath, or when someone stopped by to say goodnight.

Something about him, the quiet way he asked questions and simply *listened*, kept her talking.

"The first time I walked in here," she said, "I knew I was home. It had been on the market for ages. They were thinking of tearing it down for housing before the market crashed. Can you imagine? I'd studied for a year in California to get ordained without really knowing why, besides wanting to be a better counselor and perform weddings for gay friends, legal or not. As soon as I stepped inside The Sanctuary, all the disconnected ends and odd twists and turns just...fell into place."

She finally stopped and looked into Ryan's eyes. The silence and connection between them said more than she thought she'd ever be able to say to another person again.

They both looked up at a soft footfall and turned

to see Ryan's sister Erin, making a halfhearted effort to hide her rather knowing smile. She held one of the pieces of paper folded in half.

"I am *so* sorry to interrupt," Erin said. "Just wanted to let you know I'm heading over to the bonfire. The people I was talking to are going and offered me a ride. There and back home."

Erin stared at Ryan with her eyes wide open, and June did her best not to laugh. At some mysterious signal, everyone else was moving around again, gathering themselves up.

Their faces and the mood and everything in the world felt lighter. Including June's heart.

"I'm so glad you found something you needed tonight, Erin," she said. "You found a good bunch of people, too."

Erin nodded. "They are. I think I'll like the meetings you have here, June. You'll be seeing me again for sure."

Ryan looked the group over, becoming every inch the protective older brother who'd walked into The Sanctuary.

"You good?" he said to Erin.

"Yeah, Ry, I'm good. You asked me at home why I wanted to come here tonight. Want to read it?"

"I do. I really do."

He took the folded paper as the few remaining members of the Longest Night congregation walked up to say goodnight. By the time June spoke to them all and turned back, Ryan held Erin in a tight hug. When he let go, he gave the folded paper back and touched her shoulder, nodding.

"Okay. Thanks, kid. See you at home."

Ryan looked at June, eyes red, but smiling.

"You had me talking all night," she said. "Now tell me if *you're* okay, Ryan."

"I am. Better than I've been in a long time. What to hear what she wrote? She said it was all right for me to tell you."

He looked toward the doors to the vestibule Erin was walking toward with her new friends. June noticed a couple of the usual members of the congregation blowing out candles, turning out lights. Taking care of everything she normally did at the end of a service.

Maybe giving her a hint.

"I'd love to hear."

When his gaze met hers, June felt heat unrelated to her biological stage of life moving through her.

Maybe this heat was to remind her she was still alive after all.

"She wrote that she forgave herself," Ryan said. "For missing so many days and weeks and years. For letting herself down. For giving up on herself. She wants to let all of that go. And she wrote that she was damn proud of herself for getting through all of that and still being here."

"Sounds like good advice for all of us." June hesitated for only one quick second before she charged ahead, Erin's knowing smile bright in her mind. "Listen, I haven't gotten to hear *your* life story yet. Want to go to the solstice bonfire with me? It's quite the event on the Laconia social calendar."

Ryan ducked his head and blushed all the way to his earlobes as they walked toward the vestibule.

"I'd love to, goofy blue coat and all. And I'll tell you everything, even if I can't fit it all in tonight. But I have to ask kind of a weird question. Will they have marshmallows? Or mind if we stop and grab some? I've been craving campfire-toasted marsh-mallows all night."

June laughed out loud and Ryan joined her, the joyful sound echoing in the empty building.

Their Sanctuary.

She hoped for a whole lot more of his laughter, and his words, and everything else.

"Would you believe they have a separate smaller fire just for that?" she said as they pulled on their coats. "Graham crackers and chocolate for s'mores, too. I'll even show you how to catch the marshmal-lows on fire without burning them. Or dropping them into the ashes."

Ryan held the back of his hand to his forehead in mock-horror.

"That's *right*, the ultimate tragedy. It's about time I got that part right."

June slipped her gray-jacketed arm into his puffy blue one, thinking they might have a chance at getting way more than that right.

Together.

JASON A. ADAMS

Author of Andrew and Shichi-Go-San

A True Family
Holiday

For the misfits who find each other.

CHAPTER 1

Carrie gave sigh of relief when she saw the steel screens rattling down over the store's mall-side entrance.

Five days until Christmas, and the Northlake Mall Sears had been the scene of screaming toddlers, fighting couples, desperate husbands, harried wives. Men with wedding rings staring at her tits and making vile suggestions, and a work policy that said she had to be cheerful and polite no matter what.

The people clashed with maniacally cheerful lights and decorations, animatronic elves, three (count 'em!) Santas competing over who could sneak the most booze in between terrified children peeing on their waterproof Santa pants.

A last quick till count, and she could escape this horrid place and get back to her quiet and people-free apartment. She loved living in Atlanta, had since she first moved here six months ago, but she still wasn't used to how many people filled the city. A far cry from Mountain City, Tennessee.

And she was four hours from her family, which worked out nicely.

Carrie finished off her tepid, bitter Starbucks, grateful she'd opted for plain old coffee instead of one of the holiday sugar bombs. She didn't think she could have tolerated room temperature Candy Cane Snowball Reindeer Delight, or whatever the silly drink *du jour* was.

The store went blessedly quiet, or at least quiet*er*, when the Muzak system stopped pounding out oppressively cheerful Christmas carols. Carrie had hated those songs since she was a kid, and wondered why, in a place as culturally diverse as Atlanta, no one thought to sprinkle in a Chanukah tune or two.

Although listening to the Dreidel song over and over again might not be any better.

Carrie's feet, legs, and back ached, and she could smell herself when she pulled the cash drawer from the overworked register. The desk job hadn't prepared her for this.

A graphic designer by trade, she'd decided to pick up some extra cash—and a good excuse—working retail for the holidays. Double- and triple-time Sears wages didn't match what she made with a computer, but every little bit helped.

One particularly horrible couple were ushered toward the door by Lenny. Like herself, he was a seasonal employee. But he'd been hired for his mass. Lenny was a minor league (or whatever) pro wrestler who worked security in between pratfalls. Carrie like to tease him about the "reality" of pro wrestling, but he was a genuinely nice guy for all his Evil Wrestler stage act.

Still, no one stayed rowdy or refused to leave when six-and-a-half-feet of nearly silent mohawked African-American fury got down in their face and quietly asked them to comply with instructions.

He'd once picked her up over his head like she weighed nothing, and given her a helicopter twirl. She'd been scared, delighted, laughing like a crazy woman…and more than a little excited. She wished she wasn't so shy. Lenny didn't wear any rings, and never talked about a significant other.

And my goodness, how he did fill out a tight black t-shirt.

"An ass like that oughtta be illegal, if it's not open to the public."

Carrie jumped, blushing as she turned to see Edward standing beside her, staring thoughtfully as Lenny continued dragging shoppers to the parking lot exit out by Women's. He was close to her own height, maybe a shade closer to six feet than she was. An impeccable dresser, today he wore a pin-striped shirt with thin, polished leather suspenders. The suspenders held up a pair of zoot suit-style pants, tight-waisted and flaring out like balloons before gripping his ankles like a vise.

"Hey, Edward. You already close out Cosmetics?" She finished counting her drawer. The cash went into a bank bag with the count sheet, and she carried it toward the manager's office.

"Yeah, like half an hour ago," Edward said walking with her. "The rabble stayed away after seven-thirty or so. The sample spritzers got a little *too* dedicated this evening. It got so bad I had to toss my contact lenses. I wouldn't strike a match anywhere near the perfume counter if I was you. You've got it lucky up here in teeny-bopper clothing."

She laid the bank bag on a growing pile in the boss's office, and walked with Edward through the back to the employee's door. All she wanted was some greasy fast food, a nice cup of chamomile tea with a bourbon bracer, and bad movies in bed.

CHAPTER 2

S he did *not* want a flat tire.

Edward rubbed her shoulders as she looked down at the sadly deflated rubber on her Outback's rear wheel. All the way down. It looked like a napping bloodhound's jowls.

Carrie opened the trunk and checked the empty well. Nope, the spare that had been missing when she bought the old clunker was still gone. So much for Christmas magic.

"Let me give you a ride, sugar," Edward said, as Carrie's throat tightened up. This was one thing too much at the end of an endless shift.

"That's okay," she said, sniffing. "I'll just call a t-t-t-tow…"

And that was it. The next moment she had her head buried in her friend's shoulder while he held and rocked her sobbing body.

"Hey...hey, now... It's not that bad, sweetie. I can take you home. We'll get the Sears-O-Matic people in Auto Service to fix you up tomorrow. Be good as new."

"But I'm not working tomorrow," Carrie said, pulling out of Edward's arms and swiping furiously at her eyes. "I've got to finish a poster and flyers for Spencer's Travel. It's going to take me all day!"

"Work? On the Saturday before Christmas? Tsk, tsk, tsk. That won't do at all, my little sugarplum."

Edward stood, arms crossed, tapping his chin with one finger while he looked toward the sky. Carrie knew that look. He was plotting and scheming again.

"Oh no you don't," she said, pinching his shoulder. "It's late and I'm tired. No bars, no dance clubs!"

"Perish the thought! I think you deserve a night off. But, since I'll be running you back and forth tomorrow, at least until we get your tire fixed, I think you should accept my most generous offer of dinner, drinks, and the sofa bed."

Carrie started to say no, that she really needed to start on that poster early, but Edward had already taken her hand and was steering her toward an over-sized Ford pickup truck. Not the sort of vehicle anyone would expect a guy like Edward to drive, but he called it his only holdover from a childhood in Outer Redneckia.

"Thanks, Edward," she said, taking a tissue from her bag and honking loudly. "I can't tell you how much I appreciate this. Burger King good for you? My treat."

"Absolutely. I love me some Whopper with my vodka."

Carrie laughed, surprising herself. This was why she loved Edward. He could make her smile no matter what else was going on. And he never tried to hit on her.

They swung through a handy drive-through and bought a ridiculous amount of food. Burgers, fries, onion rings, one of each dessert. A quick stop at the package store for two bottles of Grey Goose, and they wound their way through the Atlanta traffic back to Edward's townhouse.

Carrie hauled the bags while Edward opened the door and killed the burglar alarm. She looked around, curious to see how her friend lived. They'd met three weeks ago at store orientation, and hit it off immediately. Kindred spirits, as he said.

The townhouse was another surprise. Spotlessly clean, decorated with Marvel and DC toys, movie posters from a million drive-in creature features, heavily decorated brass vases and hookahs like something out of Arabian Nights...

And not a single holiday decoration. No tree, no tinsel, no lights.

She was about to ask him about that, when her

phone buzzed in her pocket. She took it out and saw "MOM" flashing on the screen. Great. Just exactly what she needed to top the day off.

"Hi, Mom," she said, preemptively rubbing her forehead. "What's up?"

"Oh, hello dear! I'm just checking on my little chicken. Have you changed your mind about coming home for Christmas? You know everyone wants to see you."

"Mom, I told you. I have to work through the holidays. Plus, I just got a big contract to do advertising materials for—"

"That's nice, Car-Car. Oh, did I tell you about your brother's promotion? He's going to be foreman at the furniture plant! Isn't that exciting? And your nephews are just *loving* hockey. They're so talented and smart and—"

Carrie tuned the rest out until Edward came back from the kitchen with burgers on plates, fries and rings in bowls, plus a bottle and two shot-glasses.

"Gotta run. A friend and I are at dinner and the food just showed up."

"Hi, Mom!" Edward called, dropping Carrie a wink. "Let me have Carrie back, and I promise to return her in good condition."

"Oh, is that a *boy* I hear? I'm so glad, Car-Car. You really need to get—"

"Bye, Mom. I'll call you tomorrow or next day." Carried disconnected, and flopped back on the couch.

"Please tell me one of those glasses is mine."

"Absolutely, sweetie. Want me to go fetch a tumbler instead?"

"No, I'll be okay. It's just that… I don't know. I love my mom and the family, I guess, but she's never interested in *me*. It's always my brother this and her grandchildren that and did you hear about your cousin Sonnie and. And. And."

"So you're not going home for the holidays, I take it?"

"Are you kidding?" Carrie grabbed a handful of fries and the shotglass Edward had so kindly filled. "My people can be decent enough one-on-one. Some of them, anyway. But get the Holbrook clan together in a large group and things go bad. Dad and my uncles get toasted and start fighting. All the women talk about is how terrible their lives are. Mom…well, you heard. Preacher Price will come by to bless everyone and bless everyone out. Real fire and brimstone and God loves you but you're gonna burn type. I hate all the holidays, but Christmas is the worst."

"I get you, sugar," Edward said, sitting beside Carrie and putting an arm around her. "You should meet my clan. Or maybe it's Klan with a K. My mom and pop love me too, but they never stop worrying about my eternal soul, no matter how many times I tell them I'm not going to a re-education gulag."

CHAPTER 3

It was the best evening Carrie'd had in a long time. She and Edward talked the sun up, getting steadily more sloshed and honest as the night went on. They ate bad food, drank, and skipped the bad movies in favor of discussing their reasons for staying away from any sort of family gathering.

Finally, Carrie fell asleep.

Or passed out.

Whatever.

She clawed her way back to consciousness some time later, and immediately regretted it. Cruel light streamed through a crack in the drapes, shoving right through her lids, skewering her eyeballs and brain. Her tongue felt coated in coarse fur. From roadkill, judging by the taste. Someone kept beating on her head with a mallet.

"Up and at 'em, sunshine!" Oh god.

She peeled one eye open. A blurry Edward stood in front of her, a steaming plate of scrambled eggs and toast in one hand, a glass full of red froth in the other.

"Go 'way," she mumbled, burrowing deeper into the couch cushions. She'd somehow acquired a quilt, which she pulled up over her aching head.

"Sorry, girl. Time's a-wastin', and you need some of Edward Campbell's Magic Hangover Cure."

She heard him set the plate and glass on the coffee table, then the blanket was whipped away.

Edward finally badgered her into sitting up and drinking the crimson liquid. A Bloody Mary, but with a bitter undertone.

"Yuck! What's in this? Rat poison?"

"Nope, but I did crush up a couple of tablets of somethin'-somethin'. I have a pharmacist friend who slips me the occasional goodie. Don't worry," he said, holding up a hand. "It's nothing that bad. Perfectly legal when prescribed by a doctor."

And the clamp around her temples *was* easing a bit. She decided to brave the eggs, and realized she was starving. Five minutes later, the glass and the plate were empty.

"Thanks Edward," she said, glancing at her watch. "I appreci—oh, shit! Noon? I've got to go! I have to work—"

"Tut, tut. Don't you worry, my little chickadee. Doctor Eduardo snooped in your purse and found the travel agent's card. You have been reported as too ill to function, and the deadline has been pushed back a couple of days."

Carrie wished she could manage a grin that smug.

"Okay, thanks I guess. Did you call a tow truck, too?"

"All in good time. Today is a day for celebrating. I'm taking you someplace special, sweetie." The smug kept getting thicker.

"Where?" she asked, growing more suspicious.

"A nice family gathering to celebrate the holidays."

"No. *Hell* no! We talked about all that last night, or at least I think we did. I don't want my family anywhere nearby right now!"

Edward pulled her to her feet. "Not your birth family, sugar. Just wait. You'll understand. But first, girl needs some quality time with a bar of soap. Shew!"

Curious in spite of her misgivings, Carrie took Edward up on the shower, and stepped out feeling more like a living creature. Whatever had been in that drink had kicked the hangover to the curb, thank goodness. She got dressed, combed her fingers through her damp hair, and went back out to the living room.

"There she is! That's the Carrie we all know and love."

"Stow it, clown. So what's this mystery gathering all about?"

"You'll see," he said, dropping another wink. "Get your bag and let's go."

CHAPTER 4

Edward drove through Decatur, and then into Druid Hills. Past houses coated with decorations: Christmas, Chanukah, Kwanzaa, and some she didn't recognize. They finally stopped in front of a large Craftsman, completely undecorated except for a green bulb in the porch light.

"Here we are," he said, killing the truck's engine. "Mind your step getting down, and follow me."

He led her up to the heavy walnut door. Carrie heard music and voices from inside, but it all sounded cheerful. No one was yelling, nothing was breaking.

Edward knocked, then rang the bell. Nothing happened.

"Can't hear us," he said. "No worries." He

KARI KILGORE & JASON A. ADAMS

turned the knob, pushed the door open, and led Carrie into holiday chaos.

"Welcome to your new family home!" he yelled over all the noise.

Carrie stopped in the doorway, goggling. The house was filled with people of all colors, dressed in a dizzying array of clothing. Pale goths covered with Wiccan jewelry, sandy-skinned people in djellabas, some in t-shirts and jeans. Towering over the others, Lenny walked toward Carrie and Edward, wearing a multi-colored dashiki.

"Hey, little girl," Lenny said, wrapping his giant arms around Carrie and swinging her around. "You come to join the family?"

"Family?" she gasped, a little breathless. From the hug.

"Welcome home, honey!" said a woman with flaming red hair, green eyes. She was wearing lederhosen. "I'm Kristen. Kris to my family, and that means you. You must be Carrie. Edward's told us *so* much about you!"

"My girl's the next big advertising honcho!" Lenny said, still keeping Carrie's feet off the ground. "Eddie tells me you scored a big graphics deal with that travel agent over in Buckhead!"

"Put me down, you big goof!" she said, laughing and slapping Lenny's arms. "Someone needs to tell me what's going on!"

"Look around and see, sweetie," Edward said.

152

He took her by the hand again and led her through rooms full of happy people. Full of decorations. Santa statues, Star Trek Hallmark ornaments, Menorahs, Kwanzaa cards…Even a plain aluminum Festivus pole in one corner. A kid wearing a yarmulke stood chatting and drinking with an older man in a cassock. Pentacles, crucifixes, dreidels, even a three-foot-tall Krampus doll. The place looked like the Amazon Holiday page had drunk a bottle of ipecac.

"You're in Atlanta, honey," Edward said. Lenny and the redhead nodded. "This is the Island of Misfit Boys. And Girls."

"We all got our reasons for not going home," Lenny said, filling a cup with eggnog from a huge crystal punch bowl and handing it to Carrie. She knocked it back in one.

"You can tell us your story or not," Kris said, stroking Carrie's cheek. "Just know that one of the benefits of turning eighteen is you aren't stuck with your biological relatives any more."

"That's right," Edward said. "Everyone here decided at one time or another to upgrade the family situation."

Lenny set Carrie down, and took one of her shaking hands in his giant mitt.

"Home's where you decide it is," Lenny said, stroking the back of her hand with his thumb. "And the best family is the one you choose for yourself."

"We all get together the last Saturday before Christmas for a big, *happy* family get-together," Edward said, taking Carrie's other hand. "We all bring whatever holiday with us, but we celebrate all of them. Or none of them. We celebrate each other, mostly. We call it *Verum Familia*, True Family."

"That's right," said Kris. "Everyone here is special. Everyone here thinks *you're* special, Carrie. We all love you just the way you are. Will you stay and be part of my family?"

"And mine," Edward said.

"And mine?" Lenny said, voice much too soft for the huge body it came from. "Please say yes, sugarbear."

Carrie looked from one face to another.

Friends she knew, friends she'd just met, and friends she hadn't been introduced to yet.

No, not friends. Family.

A family that knew she had a big client.

A family looking at *her*.

That cared how *she* was.

Something pricked the corners of her eyes, and she noticed she was grinning like an idiot. She hugged first Edward, then Kris. Then she tried to squeeze the life out of Lenny.

She finally let the wrestler go and wiped her cheeks, still smiling.

"Got any more of that eggnog?"

KARI KILGORE

AUTHOR OF THE WORRY TRAP AND AT THE HEART OF IT ALL

Virginia's Last
Old Christmas Eve

For those who keep loved ones alive
by telling their stories

VIRGINIA'S LAST OLD CHRISTMAS EVE

Virginia Buchanan's living room hadn't been so wonderfully decorated for years. Or so wonderfully full of her family.

Her great-grandchildren had been tickled to no end at the chance to harvest a second Christmas tree the day before. A beautiful cedar brought down from the mountain above the house stood imperfect and proud, taking the place of the usual tree-farmed pine. Those had always looked too perfect to be natural to Virginia's eyes.

The calendar had cooperated with a weekend only a few days after the new year, and the weather by staying clear and fine. After spending the holidays at home, everyone had filled Virginia's heart full near to bursting by gathering for a traditional mountain Old Christmas Eve.

The sharp, fresh aroma of the cedar tree on the

fifth day of January alone took her almost all the way back to the Old Christmas of her Virginia childhood nearly a century ago.

As far back as she needed to go, anyway.

Her swarm of great-great grandbabies, joined by an ever-changing gang of grand-nieces and nephews, had spent the whole glorious day learning how to decorate the new tree in the old way. There were tricks to turning the thin spots into advantages.

Ornaments that had started the day as a pretty pinecone or a shiny green holly branch with glossy berries filled in nicely. A couple dozen bright and fancy fabric squares the size of her palm hung on wire hooks, each sewn up with hard candies inside for later.

Garlands made of every color of paper under the sun cut into rings of every shape and size snaked through the branches. Virginia was especially proud of the ones the older kids had arranged in order as the sizes and colors changed. But the chains that fit together for no reason at all besides the littlest had put them there for someone else to glue were every bit as precious.

The prettiest strings of popcorn ever strung on sturdy thread hung on the tree and along the top of the curtains and doors and pretty much everywhere else they would fasten. Her grandkids and a couple of her kids, well into their sixties themselves now, had helped with that project. The sweet smell of all that freshly popped corn still hung in the air. The white strings of her youth blended perfectly with the ones dyed red, green, purple, and even pink.

Virginia was delighted to see actual socks in every size and color taking the place of flat, store-bought stockings that had hung on her mantle for years. The only rules were folks had to fetch them out of their sock drawer, and of course they had to be clean.

She'd dropped oranges, apples, walnuts in their shells, and home-made chocolate and peanut butter fudge wrapped in sparkly colored cellophane into those socks first thing this morning.

On the mantle itself above a cheery fire, tucked in between more sprigs of holly and branches from the Christmas pine, photos of the dear and departed overlooked the cozy day.

Virginia's parents in grainy tintype stood beside her sisters and brother. Her husband Wilson, gone these twenty long years, grinned out at his family in bright and faithful color. Virginia teared up at some of the photos of family and friends taken away too young, but she was thankful that sad number remained so small.

One of the tragic photos that had been added only a few months before was of her grandson Robbie's wife. Cancer had carried Rachel away at barely forty-one, leaving Robbie heartbroken and reeling. His moving into Virginia's sprawling, empty house had been the only sensible choice as far as she was concerned.

To help care for her, certainly. But mainly so he could take care of himself for a while.

Robbie was just now making the after-dinner rounds with tall slices of dark brown apple stack cake, and two of the other grandkids followed with coffee, tea, or hot apple cider. Virginia had supervised him in baking the cake herself, getting the exact amount of rich apple butter between seven thin, molasses-flavored layers. He'd wrapped it to rest to perfection a few days ago.

Now he absolutely beamed when she took a bite, closed her eyes, and sighed.

"One of the best I've ever tasted, sweetheart. Just as soft and moist as my own mother made."

"I haven't even spiked her apple cider with bourbon yet," he said, grinning around at their family. "Don't worry, I wrote down every word of her recipe. I'll be collecting bribes later."

"Are you writing down Memaw's stories, Robbie?" said Annie, one of the great-grandkids. "I know I haven't heard all of them yet."

"Could be." He winked as he settled down beside the fire. "Now's your chance to hear some good ones. Tell them what Old Christmas is about, Memaw."

Virginia couldn't stop from laughing at the way twenty pairs of eyes all looked to her at once. Even the little ones who really did need that nap after all managed the trick.

"There's not a whole lot to tell," she said, "once you leave out my stubborn Scottish granddaddy fussing and quarreling about keeping his family's own traditions no matter what. He said it went all the way back to when the American colonies put up a fight about changing their calendars over two hundred years ago. By the time I came along, most folks in these mountains had Christmas in December. Mostly at home with our families, like you all do. But then we'd travel around and have Old Christmas, too."

One of the sleepy-eyed little girls, just about to lose the battle with naptime, piped up.

"You had presents and Santa *two* times?"

Virginia laughed along with everyone else, including the sleepyhead.

"No, honey, sorry to say. Not much more than the candies on the tree and the treats in your sweet little stockings. For us at least, we didn't have a whole lot on December 25th, either. But for Old Christmas Eve, we spent time together. A lot of people celebrate Epiphany on January 6th, when the three wise men visited with the new baby Jesus. So it makes sense that we visited each other the day before. Even if we did different things."

She sipped her cider, lost in old, old memories.

"Boys roaming around shooting off guns and

fireworks to care away evil spirits. Girls and women baking and talking and laughing, and sewing up new pillowcases for the year. We even sewed up pennies right into the seams for good luck. Old Christmas Day itself was more of a quiet time."

"There was something else," Annie said, tilting her head to one side. "Something about the animals and the gates of Heaven?"

Virginia hesitated, not sure if this was a good topic for such a happy day. Death and the afterlife—and especially those gates of Heaven—had been very much on her mind lately. That was normal for an old woman who'd already lost most people her own age.

But she didn't want to hurt Robbie. They'd spent many a long hour talking since he'd moved in, strangely linked in their mourning. He for the unfair, early loss of life, she for the slow winding down of a life long and well-lived.

His eyes were brighter than normal, but he smiled at her and nodded.

"That was two different things," Virginia said. "They said the animals in the barnyard and all over in the forest would pray when it was getting close to midnight on Old Christmas Eve. That if you went outside at the right time, you could hear them, but it was rude to listen in. Even the honeybees hummed the Psalms because they were so happy about Jesus being born."

"And the angels?" Robbie said. A tear slipped down his cheek, but he was still smiling.

Virginia blinked back her own tears. She was longing to tell her own story about an angel this evening, but not with the little ones around.

"That's one of my favorite parts. I always heard it said that the angels who guard the gates of Heaven are so busy celebrating on Old Christmas Eve that they leave their posts. For that hour right before midnight, the souls of those that were worried about their lives can walk right through. Worried because of sins in the eyes of the world, the eyes of their Lord, or in their own eyes. Makes no difference on that joyful hour. They're one and all welcomed home."

More than Robbie and Virginia wiped their eyes then, but Virginia hoped they felt as elated and relieved as she did instead of sad.

"Amen," Annie said, smiling and reaching for Virginia's hand. "There's hope for some of us yet."

Annie wasn't anywhere near the only one of the group that didn't go to church any time of the year. And like the rest, Virginia knew Annie was as sweet and good as any woman to ever draw breath.

At that benediction for everyone, the folks who would drive home that night shifted and stirred. They'd all arranged beforehand that a few would clean up and spend the night. Robbie had quietly arranged for sleepovers for some of the kids, and arranged for specific people to stay.

Virginia hated to see the little ones go, but deep inside she was relieved only adults he'd chosen were staying to hear her story.

She was glad they'd be there along with her ghosts to share her last Old Christmas Eve.

WHEN ROBBIE MADE the rounds an hour later with the seven members of Virginia's family who'd stayed, he was generous with the bourbon. Virginia took a healthy nip along with the honey in her tea. She'd gotten a lot more comfortable ignoring her doctor's orders over the last few months.

She knew she'd feel better when the evening came to an end. Ever *so* much better. But that didn't keep a rather girlish flutter of nervousness out of her belly.

"Here you go, Memaw. We're all ready when you are."

Robbie placed a pin still cool from her nightstand in her palm, then closed her fingers gently over it. He leaned down and kissed her cheek before he sat with the others.

Virginia opened her hand and turned the pin from side to side. Not much longer than a quarter, the gold gilded profile of Pallas Athene shone in the light from the fire. Goddess of victory and womanly virtue. Her face was serious, and a tall brushy crest sat atop her helmet. Virginia admitted she couldn't see the fine details as well as she could when she wore a pin just like it proudly on her lapel, opposite the simpler one that only held the letters "U.S."

But her memory of everything about that time was remarkably clear and strong.

Virginia looked past Robbie, chatting quietly with their family, some older and some younger than he was. To the wall across from her recliner that held photos as dear to her as those on the mantle in all that greenery. To a small constellation of black and white photos that stayed there all year round.

All from the same three years that loomed so large in her long life.

A woman Virginia recognized more than the wrinkled, aged one she saw in the mirror every day gazed out from the largest. Dark hair in perfect waves not quite to her chin, with a straight-sided cap pulled down to just over her raised left eyebrow. The creased top of the cap followed that jaunty angle away from her face. Smooth, firm skin, clear eyes. And a subtle smirk that matched her eyebrow perfectly.

More times than not lately, Virginia felt more like that proud, vaguely terrified girl in her late twenties than an old woman who'd just turned a hundred and one.

Surrounding her Women's Army Corps graduation photo were a dozen smaller ones from the same era. The women she trained with, the ones she traveled with to London and later France. Virginia at work, teaching women and even men how to send and receive coded transmissions. Smiling with a few of her closest friends.

And in almost all of those photos, one woman drew Virginia's eye every bit as she had during that long-ago time. Neither her vibrant red hair or her sea green eyes showed in those old photos.

They'd never faded in Virginia's mind.

She rubbed her fingertips over the bumpy, ridged, and smooth surface of the officer's pin as she had so many times over the decades.

"I've had the most wonderful day with all of you here," she said, smiling. "The best day I've had in a long, long time. I appreciate all of you for staying with me tonight. I hope you'll want to listen to one more story."

Robbie only returned her smile. He didn't know exactly what she was going to say, but he knew how much it mattered to her.

Annie's voice rose above the general noises of agreement.

"I always love to hear your stories, Memaw. Every single time."

"You're in for a treat, then," Virginia said. "No one else has ever heard this one. Only one other person knew any of it happened. She's gone now, so you'll be the only ones."

She swallowed the rest of her tea, enjoying the spicy warmth of the bourbon all the way down to her belly. Her nerves were calm and steady, and so was she.

"You've heard many a tale about my time in the Women's Army Corps. A lot of it was exciting, and a whole lot was sad and lonely. Most of it was scary, at least in the back of my mind. I made some of the best friends I've ever had during that time."

Virginia held her breath for a second, wondering if the tears would start now or later.

"I found out back before Thanksgiving that the last one I was in touch with all these years had passed."

Now. The tears would start now.

That was fine. Her family and her ghosts were there to keep her company.

"The one I want to tell you about left this life a long time before that. Lillian had a great big wonderful family like I do, so I know a lot of people loved her and remember her. What I want to tell you right now is I loved Lillian, too. I was… We were in love."

That girlish tremble was back in Virginia's belly and chest, and more in her hands than she wanted to admit. She'd never said such a thing out loud. But the seven fine men and women who'd heard her say it didn't gasp or draw back in horror. Their eyes got a little wider, and a couple of them closed their mouths right quick.

But they all looked back into her eyes, and every one with love.

"Now I don't want you to get the idea that I didn't love Wilson. I surely did, and I always will as long as I draw breath. Marrying him after the war and having our wonderful family was one of the best things I was ever blessed to do. But I know all of you are old enough to have fallen in love. And to have that one love you always wondered about. That was Lillian for me."

Everyone nodded and smiled. Virginia saw two people reach out and touch Robbie, and that made her heart feel a little lighter for talking about love and loss with his so recent and sharp.

"Lillian worked with radio equipment, repairing it and teaching women and men how to use it. So we were together a lot with me teaching the codes and all. She was beautiful, but that wasn't what drew me to her. She was smart, so *smart*. One of the funniest people I ever met, too. I don't mind telling you that she could tell a better dirty joke than any man I've ever known. I hope someone in her family wrote some of those down."

Virginia laughed with her family, and it sat

perfectly with the slow tears rolling down her cheeks.

"Lillian was from up north, around Boston, and she loved my mountain accent. Said it made her toes curl, she did. See, we only knew each other for a few weeks before we fell hard. If we'd gone our different ways after training, I don't know if we would have fallen quite so deep. But we were together the whole time, the last three years of the war."

A couple of the women were crying now, too, along with Robbie. Virginia wasn't even a little bit surprised to see Annie's brow draw down in curiosity.

Virginia sighed and closed her eyes for a second.

"I did think about it, yes. Staying with her. Maybe staying in France, hard as times were there with so much to rebuild. I would have missed the mountains and my family something fierce. But we would have been together.

"I wanted to at least try, and I tried to talk to Lillian about it when the war was over. Her family was close, too. They were religious, like my family, but something had happened with one of her cousins and the church when she was little. She never would talk much about it, but I know it scared her deep down inside. We had to be careful all those years, but she felt safer somehow, even in the middle of a war. She loved me, but once that time was over, she was too scared."

"You know what happened to her, though," Robbie said. "She got married and had kids?"

"That was what we were supposed to do." Virginia smiled and shook her head. "I don't mean it like that, most of us *wanted* to. You have to remember it was the 1940s, and we'd just lived through another terrible war. So many people hurt or killed. All of us, men and women alike, wanted to get back to our normal lives. Normal then meant work for the men and babies for the women."

She looked around at each precious person, each one part of her very own flesh and blood. She gazed into each pair of eyes until they smiled back.

"Lillian married not long after I did. She and her husband stayed in Boston, and they had even more children than we did. We sent each other pictures every year, and letters. She was very happy, just like I have been. Her Patrick was a good man. I was almost as heartbroken when he passed as when my Wilson did."

Virginia smiled, and she knew a blush was climbing up to her cheeks. In her heart she knew they weren't, but the words still felt like a betrayal of her husband.

"I thought about that little French chalet sometimes over the years. Our *petite maison*. When I was tired or sad, or Wilson was out of town. Even more once both our husbands were gone. All our kids grown. I mentioned it to her in my letters sometimes. She always sent me little pictures she'd find in a book or magazine of cottages in the French countryside.

"But she always kept that fear, even when we were together. So afraid she'd condemned her eternal soul for loving me. She had a happy marriage, all those beautiful babies. Confession week after week. Hours and hours of good work in the church and all around her community. None of that made my sweet Lillian's fear go away."

Virginia hadn't realized her voice had gone hoarse and weak until Robbie and Annie were at her side. Annie poured the tea and he added the bourbon and the honey.

She sometimes felt short of breath these days, but this was her last story to tell. She would see it through to the end. She took a good sip and a long, deep breath. Virginia held up the officer's pin, Pallas Athene glinting forever young and strong.

"We couldn't give each other rings or a home, and we couldn't give each other babies. All we could do was give each other these pins we'd worn near our hearts in a dangerous time, and a hug and a kiss goodbye."

"You never saw her again?" Annie said, wiping at her eyes.

"I never did. We talked about it back in France,

and in our letters sometimes. We never did, though. I didn't tell you this to make you sad, now. Not a bit of it. I thought I might stay by myself my whole life long once I left Lillian, but I met Wilson only a year later. I've loved my life, and I love every one of you.

"I wanted you to hear the story of Lillian and Virginia. I hope she told someone in her family or one of her friends, but I'll never know for sure. What I *do* know now is our love story won't fade away when I do. That comforts me more than you can ever imagine."

JUST LIKE EARLIER WHEN she'd finished talking about the unguarded gates of heaven, everyone understood it was time to go and get ready for bed. Virginia accepted their hugs and kisses, their whispered words of sympathy and love. She drank it all in like the countless blessings she'd had throughout her long life.

Robbie had done her proud knowing exactly who should be there to hear this story.

He was the last one she saw, helping her get into bed and pull the thick quilts up under her arms. Robbie sat beside her and picked up the golden pin from her nightstand. He stared at it as he turned it over in his hands.

"Did Lillian know about the gates of heaven on Old Christmas Eve?"

"I don't know, honey. I might have told her about it in all the hours we spent talking and talking, but I don't remember."

He stared at the pin for a few more seconds, then he stared into her eyes. Virginia held his gaze, waiting to see what he'd find.

She thought she knew.

"Are you afraid, Memaw?"

"No honey. I'm not afraid at all."

He held out the pin. Virginia took it, and he held her hand in both of his.

"Are you ready?"

"I'm ready. Are you going to be all right, Robbie?"

He didn't cry this time, but his eyes were sad.

"I'll miss you something awful. But if you're ready, I'll be okay. Can you do…something for me? When you get there?"

"If I can, I will. I promise."

Robbie shifted his hands until his wedding band flashed silver in the low light. He took a deep breath.

"If you see her… Rachel, I mean. If you see Rachel, can you make sure she knows the way? Make sure she knows she can walk right through?"

Virginia laid her hand against his cheek.

"Don't you worry one second about Rachel.

She's exactly where she wants to be. If I see her, I'll give her your love."

He nodded, his lips pressed tight together.

"I helped her," he said. "In the end. When it hurt so bad and the drugs didn't work anymore. It was the hardest thing I ever had to do, giving her those pills. Watching her close her eyes for the last time. But it wasn't nearly as hard as watching her suffer."

He smiled, and it looked like the bright sun coming out from behind the darkest cloud.

"I'd help you if you needed me to. But I think you know the way just fine. I love you, Memaw."

"I love you, Robbie. It's all going to be all right. For all of us."

WHEN VIRGINIA SAW HER, she looked like Pallas Athene in her gorgeous, blazing glory. Her hair shone fiery and red, her eyes flashed with emerald flame.

Lillian stepped forward and took Virginia's hand.

And all the fear that had ever been in the world was but a memory.

And the only thing left to them when they passed through together was love.

Convenience Store
CHRISTMAS

To all the family members we weren't born with.

CHAPTER 1

Oh, the traffic outside was frightful. But the tunes inside delightful.

Stuart Michaelson finished spraying faux snow across the base of the Stuart's Stop 'N Shop frontage glass walls, bringing it up the sides a little as he hummed along with The Waitresses and *Christmas Wrapping*. The spray-on variety was the only snow anyone in Atlanta was likely to see, unless a stray flake or two shut down the city some extra-cold night.

Up at the register, Susie sat with some gigantic book about long-dead people propped on the counter, sipping from an oversize mug full of hot cider so spiced that Stuart's eyes burned even at this distance. *Interesting* was the best way to describe how the aroma of her wassail went with the usual smells of strong coffee and hot dog that always filled the place.

Susie was one of his two helpers—his on-the-book helpers—and the one who'd been with him the longest. A perky nineteen-year-old, she studied dead people at the college up the way, and always seemed to be cramming for some test or other. This time, it was midyear finals. Last push before she headed home at the end of the week to somewhere in Tennessee to spend the holidays with her folks.

Five-five and mighty alive, Susie always put extra effort into clothing that showed how much she didn't care. For all her eye-rolling disdain for the world, her ponytail had changed from its usual pink to a more festive scarlet in keeping with the season. Good kid.

Mike, Stuart's other helper, had already left for his uncle's place in Tahoe.

Stuart himself would be right here with Bobby for the next three weeks, keeping the store open from six in the morning to eleven at night, Christmas Eve and Day included.

Not like he had any family left to gather with.

Not that he would've anyway. Family get-togethers were always trouble.

He had his store.

Bobby had his cat.

Behind Stuart, Bobby shuffled uneasily from foot to foot, his sneakered feet coated in the dull silver of brand-new duct tape, the only thing holding his ancient kicks together. At least his brown corduroy pants and blue work shirt were relatively new. Stuart had bought them last month, dirtied them up a little in a park, and given them to his pal.

Bobby wouldn't let Stuart buy him clothes. But stuff Stuart "found?" That was okay.

"Please, Mr. Stuart—I mean Stuart—do you want me to wash all the white powder away, please?"

He'd brought Bobby in from the streets a few months ago, when the strange homeless man's cat Pete had broken his leg. He'd cut a deal with Bobby. Wash the windows, sweep the floors. Wash his hide from time to time in the standalone shower Stuart had installed in the stock room.

Do all that, and Bobby and Pete could stay as long as they needed to. Stuart did his best to pay Bobby, but the odd duck refused more than the occasional dollar bill or handful of coins. Stuart had finally convinced him he and Pete could browse the shelves for grub, as long as neither went overboard.

Ever since, Bobby and Pete lived behind the store, in a plywood shed Stuart had convinced the code inspectors was for extra supplies. He'd tried to get Bobby to crash at his place, but Bobby said he couldn't sleep indoors. Got too anxious. Felt trapped. But he could handle the shed, which was enough like a dumpster.

Stuart did his best, and his best would have to do.

He was pretty sure Doreen, his most frequent health code snoop, knew the deal. But she also absolutely refused to look inside Bobby's castle.

She also never seemed to notice any paw prints on the sales counter, bless her.

"Nah, not this time, Bobby. You can wash the outside, for sure. But leave this side of the glass alone until I tell you, okay? It's part of the holiday decorations."

Stuart straightened up, leaning back with his hands on his spine until he felt the welcome pops run all the way from tail to hackles.

The convenience store which comprised the Michaelson Realm was always as spotless as Stuart and Bobby could keep it, but with the big December festivities on the way, they'd gone the extra mile.

Plastic candy canes big enough for Goliath's walking sticks hung from the ceiling, along with dreidels the size of cash registers. Strings of lights in Kwanzaa greens and reds blinked around the edges of the ceiling and along the tops of stock cabinets, reflecting up from the mirror-polished speckled white tiles on the floor.

Stuart wasn't much for holiday hoo-hah, but

plenty of customers were. Besides, it was nice to have the occasional change to the day-in, day-out.

The entrance doors whooshed open, letting in an arctic blast that might have dipped into the fifties.

"Hey, young Bobby! How you do?"

Stuart didn't need to see the puff of white hair or the mahogany face under the red feathered chapeaux. That voice, full of pure Old Atlanta, said it all.

Bobby muttered something more or less polite, and shuffled toward the stockroom door. He still hadn't gotten the hang of people, outside of Stuart and Susie, who'd been none too pleased when Bobby joined them, but had since sort of taken the older man under her much younger wing and was now his de facto big sister.

"Hey there, Miz Annabelle. How are you this fine day?" Stuart said, dropping his empty snow can in the trash and wiping his hands on his pocket rag. "Out hunting your Christmas goose?"

Through the glass, he could see her whale of a car, a Lincoln Continental at least forty years old and at least as brightly waxed as the Stop 'N Shop's floors. And wondered yet again how she managed to drive the thing. The old dear couldn't possibly see over the steering wheel.

"Goose? Now why would I cook goose when my two grandbabies, those that have Fat Bubba's Barbecue, already got the grill full of good hardwood and a gret big ol' chunk of cow ready to roast?" She laughed, showing a set of dazzling white, and most likely store-bought teeth. "You and young Bobby ought to come down and fix a plate on the day. That boy needs to get some meat on him."

Stuart laughed along and carried Miz Annabelle's purchases to the counter so Susie could ring the old gal up. The usual salt and vinegar chips, a diet co-cola, and a *National Enquirer* (got to keep an eye on all them rascals).

Susie took Miz Annabelle's money and starting putting things in a plastic bag. She felt the chips, frowned, and held up a finger.

"Mr. Michaelson? These feel all crunched up. Maybe you should get Miss A a different bag."

"Ain't a thing wrong with—" Miss Annabelle started, but that finger with its black-polished nail jutted even more fiercely.

"Okay, okay," Stuart said, holding up his hands in surrender. "Sit tight, Miz Annabelle."

He went to get another bag of acid chips. He saw Bobby peeking around the stockroom door, and a much smaller gray face closer to the floor. Pete best not sneak out while customers were in the store.

He found what he judged to be acceptable potato chips, and turned back toward the register. He saw Susie leaned way over the counter while Miz Annabelle nodded, those LED teeth flashing in a broad grin that took about thirty years off her seamed face.

Now what was all that about?

"Here you go," he said, putting the new chips in the bag. "What are you two plotting and scheming?"

"Don't worry about it, Mr. Michaelson," Susie said, turning back to her tome. *Advance of the Visigoths in the Western Roman Empire,* this one was. Stuart got a headache just reading the title.

"Lady business," Miz Annabelle said, patting his arm. "Don't you fret none, young man."

CHAPTER 2

"Mrow?"

A gray-furred body leapt up beside the cash register and shoved its head under Stuart's hand.

"Dammit, Pete. You know you can't be in here," Stuart muttered, scratching as Pete turned his head this way and that, making sure the dumb human got all the right spots.

He was watching the front while Susie took a break from the books to restock the soda cooler. Bobby worked around her, plying his squeegee along the cooler doors until the glass turned plumb invisible.

Odd duck or not, the man sure could clean windows. And floors. Damn shame Stuart hadn't been able to prize anything about his family or history out of him. Poor guy would be stuck spending Christmas at the store with Stuart.

Susie came back up front as Bobby traded his squeegee for the Nixon-era rotary buffer and got to work polishing a floor already smoother than Teflon. As soon as the ancient machine started up, Pete hissed and made a break for the stockroom, scooting a stack of lottery blanks backward to the floor as he peeled out.

"You about ready to head for the hills?" Stuart asked. For once, Susie didn't have a book resting on the counter. Exams must be over. Day after tomorrow, he'd be on his own. Except for Bobby.

"Yeah, just about," she said, flipping her red ponytail over her shoulder. "In fact, if you have any errands you need to run for the store, you might want to do them today while I can cover. I *might* be here tomorrow, but maybe I'll have to leave a day early. Something might come up, you know?"

"Probably not a bad plan, Suze." Yeah, he could stand to pick up a bucket of floor polish. Maybe some more window cleaner, a case of coffee filters…

Heck. Be good to stock up on all the consumables, just in case things got crazy while his helpers were away.

"Too bad you can't get a tree for Bobby."

Stuart stopped staring at the list behind his eyes.

"Huh? A tree?"

"Sure." Susie smiled as Bobby worked the floor buffer like a born pro. "Maybe not a huge tree, but something you could put some lights on, and maybe a star on top. Who knows if Bobby's ever had a real Christmas tree?"

Stuart rubbed his chin, thinking.

"Well, why not? Wouldn't fit in his shed, but maybe in the back..."

Ponytail flew as Susie shook her head.

"No way, boss. My folks have cats. Tillie and Weasel. Every year the pops puts up a silly huge tree, covers it with ornaments, and then cusses a blue streak all the way through New Years because of how the cats climb up in the tree and knock all the ornaments off. All that stuff is just toys to them."

"Hm."

Stuart thought about Bobby, spending Christmas in his simple shed with only Pete for company.

"You know what, Suze? An errand run sounds like a fine idea. Things are pretty slow today. You good to cover for a few hours? Might be a little longer, but I'll call if I don't think I'll be back before seven or so. You can keep an eye on Bobby. Make sure he doesn't polish all the tile down to the dirt."

"Sure, Mr. Michaelson. Maybe I'll order in a pizza."

"You do that," he said, dropping a couple of twenties on the counter and paying more attention to his plans than her. "Go ahead and give the delivery driver a good tip. And save me a slice."

CHAPTER 3

S tuart got back to the store at a quarter to seven, patting himself on the back for making good time.

He'd been to every discount pet shop in a five mile radius, and the back of his truck was loaded down with bags.

A stop at the mall had taken a little longer, given the distance he'd had to park from the entrance this close to the Big Day, but he'd found a spot near his *other* stop, so that had all worked out.

He parked near the doors, made sure the tarp covered everything in the bed of the truck, and went inside, smiling as *Jack Frost and the Hooded Crow* greeted him.

Whatever she was learning up at the college, Stuart had taken it on himself to teach Susie about Jethro Tull.

And Susie was alone. Had Bobby gone out back, or disappeared on one of his occasional walkabouts?

"Hey, Mr. Michaelson, Get everything you need?"

Susie's feet were propped on an upturned milk crate as she leafed through the latest tattoo magazine. She looked somehow even more bored and disdainful of life in general than usual.

Stuart's hackles stood at attention. What was she up to?

"Yeah, I did. Where's Bobby at? And why is your smugmometer on high?"

"No idea what you're talking about, boss man. Bobby might be back in the stockroom. Maybe. How would *I* know?" She smiled lazily. Flipped another page in her magazine. Crossed her feet the other way.

Stuart's eyes narrowed. Nothing good could come of an attitude like that.

Before he could do...something...the stockroom door opened and Bobby came toward the counter at, if not a run, at least a fast shuffle, trailing tails of duct tape from his sneakers.

"Please Mr. Stuart, it wasn't me or Pete, I promise, please!"

Bobby looked cleaner than usual, his face pink with fresh scrubbing and flushed with red.

"Whoa now, Bobby. What wasn't you?" He

turned to squint at Susie some more. "*What* wasn't him, Susan Marie Gardener?"

"Ooo," she said, the smug little smuggle. "All three names! I must be in real trouble, huh, Papa?"

"I can always find a new employee, you know."

She smirked. "Another employee who'd let you run off to waste a whole day while she sat here and helped you make rent?"

Bobby tugged at his sleeve. "Please, Mr.—I mean Stuart. Pete and me didn't do anything in the back."

Stuart looked from Bobby's worried face to Susie's grin. He really should send both of them packing, dammit.

Finally, he threw up his hands. "Come on and show me what you didn't do, Bobby." He stopped at the front door to switch off the red neon *OPEN* sign and throw the deadbolt. Then he jabbed his own finger at his soon-to-be-ex-employee. "And *you* come right along with us, missy."

"Sure thing, boss man. Be glad to."

Susie stood up, stretched a big stretch, and sauntered back toward the stockroom, straightening that bright red ponytail that really wasn't professional at all.

Bobby shuffled along behind Stuart, hands wringing over and over.

And it had started out as such a good day.

Susie turned to face him and Bobby, leaning

against the wall beside the door, hands in the pockets of her ripped jeans.

"Well?" Stuart said. "Are you going to…what *is* that?"

Stuart smelled something coming from behind the stockroom door. Something that filled his mouth with water.

"I didn't do it!" Bobby whined behind him.

Susie put a black-nailed hand on the doorknob and pushed the door open.

"Why don't you see for yourself, Mr. Michaelson?"

Stuart's jaw headed for his shoes.

The stockroom was gone.

All the boxes and crates of dry goods had been pushed against the walls, leaving the center of the floor, a space nearly as large as the store out front, empty.

Except for a couple of couches, and a long table loaded down with food.

A puff of white hair under a pointy elf hat instead of her usual red marked Miz Annabelle as she went from one tray of ribs to another of roast beef to one that held bratwursts far superior to anything that had ever graced Stuart's rolling warmers out front.

Behind her, two enormous men, at least six-four, who looked so much alike they had to be twins, from gleaming shaved heads to biceps bigger than his leg moved along doing exactly what she told them. Elephants obeying a mouse.

At one end of the open space sat an electric fireplace shaped like a certain famous space villain's helmet, glowing with faux flames. On a rug in front lay a gray pile of laziness, next to a pile of shredded cow that looked to have started out much larger.

"Merry whatever you celebrate, Mr. Michaelson," Susie said, "And you too, Bobby."

She hugged them one after another, while the savvy business owner and street-smart survivor tried to dredge up anything useful to say.

Stuart's eyes smarted, from the sterno under the serving trays, probably. He blinked away the sting as Miz Annabelle came over with her own hugs.

"Merry Christmas, young man," she said, smacking a lipstick rose on his cheek. "You and young Bobby got no call to miss Christmas dinner, you just gonna get it a little bit early."

"Yeah," Susie said. "I know you both. You'll sit in this store all day, every day until me and Mike come back. So you're just gonna have to sit down and have Christmas with us. Or Hanukah, or whatever."

Stuart blinked faster. And felt his mouth widen as a frog tried to fill his throat.

"Susie…Miz Annabelle…I…"

"You *nothing*," Miz Annabelle said, patting his arm. "You go sit. Then you're gonna eat. My grandbabies make the best damn barbecue between here and Timbuktu."

He turned to his friend. "What say, Bobby? Will you stay and have some supper with us?"

Bobby stared at the ground as his duct-taped feet shuffled, but Stuart thought he saw a smile.

"Can Pete stay too, please?" Almost a whisper, but not a refusal to stay inside with people.

"You bet," Susie said, taking Bobby's hand and leading him to a chair. "Come on, Mr. Michaelson."

"Not just yet." Stuart wiped a hand across his eyes. "Miz Annabelle? You reckon one of your grandbabies could help me bring a few things in from my truck?"

The old woman paused from adding another pound of food to a plate tested to its limits. "'Course they will. Jeremy, you go on now and fetch what young Stuart tells you."

"Yes'm," said one of the two interchangeable giants. "You show me what, then show me where." Another wide grin added to the grins already filling the room. "Then we gonna eat until you cry, Mr. Michaelson."

Ten minutes later, the Christmas tree Stuart had bought for Bobby and Pete stood beside the electric fire, covered with the hundred or more cat toys he'd picked up to stand in for traditional ornaments.

Bobby sat between Susie and Stuart, all three of them with a plate full of more barbecue, corn, mashed potatoes, and greens than any four humans could manage. They ate, trying not to choke with laughter whenever another cat toy came flying off the tree, revealing a pair of wide green eyes in the shadows behind.

Miz Annabelle and her grandbabies stayed and ate dinner with the Stop 'N Shop family and kept all the plates full until Stuart begged for mercy.

Susie blushed—actually *blushed* as red as her dyed ponytail—when Jeremy's brother Jonah said her spiced cider would make an angel beg for more.

Midnight was in its grave by the time all the trays were packed back into the twins' van, left-overs shared out or stored in the store's cooler, and foam cups filled with cider for Miz Annabelle and her grandbabies to take home.

Stuart waved after Jeremy and Jonah as they drove away, and walked Miz Annabelle to her green tank of a car.

"I don't know how to thank you, ma'am," he said. "I sure do appreciate—"

"Hush now," she said, patting his arm. "You march right back in yonder and thank that young girl in there. Was her told me you and Bobby ain't got no people. Me and mine feel blessed we could share a little with y'all."

Stuart tried, but all he could do was nod and wave as she got in her car and drove away.

He walked back through the store, brushing his fingernails over the crystal-clear glass-fronts.

He hoped the Roman coin set got to Susie's parents' house in time. Not high-quality coins, but they sure were old.

Bobby would just have to swallow his pride and accept the new sneakers waiting for him under the tree.

Susie met him at the stockroom door, finger to her lips.

"Come here and check it out, Mr. Michaelson," she whispered, taking his hand and pointing at the couch nearest the still-glowing electric fire.

Bobby lay curled up on his side, Pete riding his shoulder.

Both of them were sound asleep.

Stuart pulled Susie from the room, softly shut the door.

"You heading back home tomorrow?" he said as they walked toward the exit. "Better get back to your place and grab some sleep yourself. Bad time of year to be driving tired."

"Yes, Papa," she said, rolling her eyes. "Don't worry, I won't get myself killed and leave you without your minion."

Then she surprised him with a huge bear hug.

"Merry Christmas, Mr. Michaelson. And tell Bobby for me, okay? And make sure he and Pete get enough to eat? I'll be back on the thirtieth to help out with New Years, I promise."

And then she was gone.

Damn good kid.

Stuart stared across the empty parking lot, then went back inside the empty store.

And didn't feel the least bit alone.

He went behind the counter and flipped on the store's music box, starting on the day's paperwork and whistling along while The Waitresses did their song about how a solo Christmas turned out to be not so solo in the end.

KARI KILGORE

AUTHOR OF ODDS AND ENDINGS AND INTENTIONS

The Magic Cat of the Hidden Springs Inn and Spa

For Zortea

Who seems to be put together out of spare parts
but her heart works better than most people's do

CHAPTER 1

As far as Henry Satterfield was concerned, the owners of the Hidden Springs Inn and Spa had clearly found the line when it came to tasteful holiday decorations. And then promptly jumped over that line and kept running, in matching pairs of red and green bedazzled high heeled boots.

Five fully decorated Christmas trees dominated the broad lobby, each highlighting a different style that did not coordinate with the others. The biggest was a perfectly shaped Fraser Fir, with the stiff, stubby leaves loaded down with every variety of non-traditional ornament available. Dark, modern colors, LED lights that oozed from one color to the next, not a scrap of tinsel to be seen. At least that one smelled good, fresh and green.

Surrounding that were what Henry thought of as

the Especially Smelly Ghosts of Christmas Past, from a Nineties department store special that came pre-decorated, a fake bendy limbed Seventies version reeking of cigarettes, all the way back to an honest-to-goodness aluminum model that reeked of other things, each loaded with decade-appropriate ornaments and potentially hazardous lighting.

The only tree Henry secretly loved was the one the inn's current owners–Suzie and Lloyd Fletcher– had given him complete freedom with. The Fletchers had asked him to pick and decorate something none of the other inns and hotels in the quaint little tourist town would have.

Henry had done a spectacular job with that one, and he wasn't the only one to say so. A brand new, extremely trendy and gorgeous solid black tree, tall and narrow, in a corner by itself. Intense violet, indigo, and blood-red lights sparkled against silver ornaments of every shape and size. Guests and Hidden Springs residents alike were drawn to that tree like goth moths to an inky black flame the second they walked through the jingle bell-laden door.

Another adjustment Henry had talked the Fletchers to making over the five years he'd worked school vacations here was adding other traditions. Besides his delightfully dark tree (which would pull double-duty at Halloween), the room held traditional and modern menorahs for Jewish guests alongside Kwanzaa displays with red, green, and black candles. Groovy old peace signs and doves dug out from the same basement storage crate as the aluminum tree competed with repurposed disco balls from a decade later.

He'd even managed to turn up the old pagan traditions with extra holly, acorns, and oak leaves to go with the dizzying array of crosses and stars and praying angels.

Of course when the Fletchers added in enough glitter and snowflakes and Santas to stock a department store, no one was likely to get bent out of shape over one religious tradition or another.

Lloyd Fletcher came bustling through just then, humming a perfectly in-tune version of *Deck the Halls* just as loud as his voice would go. Still, it was a bit jarring against the slow and ponderous choir version of *O Little Town of Bethlehem* playing over the stereo. Henry gratefully took the excuse to turn the "music" off.

Lloyd was almost a foot shorter than Henry's lanky six-foot-two, and just about as round and jolly as the Santa-man himself. All the lobby's overly cheery lights and sparkles gleamed off of his head, and a holiday-induced grin decorated his round face. Henry figured he looked downright gloomy in comparison, with his short brown hair and goatee emphasizing his own longish face.

"Are you *sure* you don't mind staying, Henry?"

he said for at least the twentieth time in the last hour. "Your folks are only a couple of hours away. Plenty of time to get there before that special order Christmas Eve snowstorm rolls in."

"I volunteered, Mr. Fletcher. Remember? I could use the extra cash and the quiet time to catch up on my reading. My brain needs a break from math and engineering. Especially if I get to chow down on those cookies."

Mr. Fletcher looked down and actually drew back, apparently surprised he was carrying a holly-shaped plate full of fresh chocolate chip, peanut butter, and sparkly pastel sugar cookies.

"Well, maybe not *all* of them," Mr. Fletcher said. "Someone might stop by yet."

He tucked the plate among the piles of oranges, tangerines, apples, and nuts already displayed on the tall check-in desk. There was enough room for any surprise guests to sign in on the electronic tablet, but only just. A smaller table off to the side held coffee, hot water for tea, and a big copper pot full of fragrant spiced apple cider steaming away over a hot plate.

"I think we've got enough out here to feed Santa and all the elves," Henry said. "Mrs. Fletcher already told me to bring the fudge out once it cools. And that she left enough food in the kitchen to feed me and the hundred guests who won't be showing up on Christmas Eve in a snowstorm."

Mr. Fletcher grasped his hands together under his chin.

"Oooooh, she made that New England fudge, didn't she? The brown sugar kind. I never can remember what it's called."

"She did, and she reminded me to tell you to keep your hands off. She's got some packed up in the car and ready to go. Speaking of go…"

This time Mr. Fletcher jumped as if one of Santa's elves had goosed him a good one. He glanced wide-eyed at his wrist watch.

"Suzie's gonna kill me. If you're sure, I'll get going then." He raised his voice and called over his shoulder. "Ms. Zee! Come out here and say goodnight!"

A jingle sounded from upstairs, then came pounding down like a herd of miniature elephants wearing bells on their collars. A nine-pound gray tabby cat with a crooked tail, tiny head, short legs, and long body shouldn't make that much noise. But Zortea, the official Hidden Springs Inn and Spa Greeter and Rodent Control Squad, managed every time.

Zortea thundered into view with a musical burble, irregular tail so high it lay nearly flat along her back. She twisted around Mr. Fletcher's legs until he picked her up. The cheerful burble instantly turned into an extremely silly and non-threatening humming growl.

"I know you don't like it when we pick you up, Fussybritches," Mr. Fletcher cooed, holding the offended feline against his chest. "I just had to say *Meowy* Christmas, Zortea. Ting-zilla. Zang-teeah."

Henry had been around dogs and cats his entire life, and he knew how many goofy nicknames they could accumulate. But he'd never heard anything like the ever-growing collection people seemed driven to bestow upon Zortea.

"The cats at this inn are magic, you know," Mr. Fletcher said, smiling at Henry. "Suzie and I aren't the only ones who met and fell in love right here in this lobby over the years."

The last thing Henry needed tonight was more advice about his rickety love life. That was one of the best reasons for avoiding his perpetually honeymooning parents, not to mention all of his happily married siblings and cousins.

"I always heard it was ghosts, Mr. Fletcher."

"Well, maybe the cats can *see* ghosts. Either way, it's the truth. You take care of Henry now, Tiffle-zee." Mr. Fletcher deposited Zortea on the rug depicting Santa's sleigh and all nine reindeer, then stepped behind the desk to give Henry a quick hug. "I know you want your peace and quiet, but I hope someone does stop in and stay for the night. I worry about you getting lonely."

Henry smiled and waved toward the door.

"I'll be perfectly fine here with Zortea the magic

cat. Go! You're going to get me in trouble with your missus!"

One more hug, and Mr. Fletcher was gone.

Henry sighed as he reached down to rub the cat's back. She immediately resumed singing to herself. He got up, got himself a mug of spiced cider and one of each kind of cookie, and settled onto the snowflake-patterned couch with his e-reader. After a few somewhat painful circles, Zortea settled down onto his shoulder and started purring.

He changed the playlist from A Special Brand of Traditional Holiday Torture to a list of his own: Holiday Songs He Could Actually Tolerate. He smiled at Vince Guaraldi's mellow *A Charlie Brown Christmas* floating through the air, as light and fantastic as the snow he could see starting outside the window.

He hoped anyone who did get caught in the storm would stop at one of the big chain hotels on the interstate rather than making their way to the inn.

A little bit lonely for Christmas Eve?

Sure.

But a thousand and one times better than his parents down in Asheville, and their overstuffed, overheated, and overly full of noisy people holiday crowd.

"You and me, Jingle-zee. You and me."

CHAPTER 2

Steve Lake swore under his breath as the time of arrival on the GPS crept up another ten minutes. At this rate, the last fifty miles of the drive were going to take longer than the first three-hundred-fifty.

A featureless white landscape stretched in all directions, unmarked by minor inconveniences like the shape of the interstate highway he was trying to travel. His sedan's wiper blades did their best, but they simply weren't designed to shove huge wedges of snow away over and over again. The fact that just as much snow covered the windshield on every return trip of the wipers didn't improve matters.

The car was warm enough, thank goodness, but the defrost set on high was drying Steve's contacts out until they felt like jagged little shards of eyeball glass. He forced his hands to relax on the wheel and rotated his shoulders.

He wasn't sure if the smell of overcooked gas station coffee on his breath or the nervous sweat rising up from his armpits was worse. His growling stomach would have greatly preferred to have something else for comparison. Especially if that something was unhealthy and absolutely delicious stress-relief food. His mom's spicy macaroni and cheese, maybe, or his father's fresh-baked gooey cinnamon rolls.

A few tractor trailers joined him on this insane voyage through snow globe hell. He could barely make out one a ways in front of him by the high taillights. Another behind him kept getting closer, but Steve was afraid to speed up much.

His wheels kind of fit in the deep ruts left by the truck ahead. Sort of. The sedan slid from side to side way too much for his comfort.

He'd turned the stereo off a few slow, anxious miles back so he could concentrate. But now his ears were begging for anything to break up the low, crunching hum of his tires and the slushy whoosh of the wipers.

Weren't there *any* exits down here at the tail end of Virginia? He would have sworn he hadn't seen one for at least a hundred miles, but that couldn't be right. He'd made this drive dozens of times over the last five years since he'd moved from East Tennessee to Washington, DC.

His current blazing speed of twenty-three miles an hour might explain the problem.

He'd so wanted to be home with his family tonight, and he'd expected to be more than an hour ago. Besides missing them more than usual since he hadn't been able to make the trip for Thanksgiving, Steve needed a good dose of home-cooked comfort. A rotten breakup in the middle of November hadn't exactly gotten his holiday season off to a spectacular start.

A flash of green to his right, too big to be one of the crawling mileage markers, made Steve's heart jump into his throat.

Could it be?

Might it be?

Yes! An exit!

He hadn't paid any attention to the small towns through here on his drives before, since he was so close to home. But all of a sudden, the unknowns of Hidden Springs, Virginia, sounded like paradise right here off the interstate.

Steve put on his turn signal and slowed even more, watching for a ridge of snow built up in his path. He'd driven in more than enough snowstorms to understand the general procedure. But this monster had taken him by surprise when he was already tired from the trip and ready to be home.

Rain in Washington and rain in Johnson City, Tennessee, the forecast had said. And that was probably true.

The higher elevation through the mountains had other ideas on this Christmas Eve.

For once, Steve was glad the snowplows didn't seem to have made an appearance yet. The snow was thick on the off-ramp, but he didn't have to crash through a plow-moat. The tire noise dropped to a whisper, draining a whole lot of the stress out of his neck and shoulders.

He could still skid into a tree or off one of the unfamiliar small-town roads. But he wouldn't have several tons of semi bearing down on top of him.

He followed the gentle curve, trying to watch the suggestion of a road and read the snow-speckled blue signs at the same time. The first listed gas stations. Full tank of gas, so no. Food? No decent restaurant would be open in this mess on Christmas Eve. Pass.

Accommodations! Two big chain hotels, both probably booked solid in this storm. Steve squinted, trying to catch the text on a third logo that promised it was only 0.3 miles away.

The Hidden Springs Inn and Spa, complete with a cartoon image of steaming hot water. Steve groaned and closed his eyes for a quick second.

He didn't care one bit whether that meant a commercial hot tub, a hotel bathtub, or an actual hot spring. He wouldn't mind if the inn cost ten times what any of the chains did.

He couldn't think of anything he'd rather do than soak this rotten drive away. He'd call his parents and break the bad news once he was able to pry his fingers loose from the steering wheel.

They wanted him home as badly as he wanted to be there, but he knew they'd understand.

Steve simply couldn't face one more mile in a freak blizzard tonight.

"Please, oh please, kind sir. Tell me you have room at your inn for one more wandering soul tonight."

CHAPTER 3

Henry jumped like he was the one goosed by a mischievous little elf when Zortea leapt from his shoulder to his thigh with no warning. She continued onto the floor with a cheery chirp and jingle, reminding him he'd need to take that bell off so she could go hunting tonight.

Two hours? He tapped the surface of his watch, certain his e-reader had lost track of the time as badly as he had.

Nope, it was indeed eight in the evening. Christmas Evening, to be exact. He'd gotten so far into his seasonally appropriate zombie apocalypse novel that he'd forgotten where he was, and why.

Now Zortea stood on the reindeer rug with her head tilted, almost like a tiny little striped dog. She chirped, going from low to high exactly like a person asking a question, then went galloping toward the front door.

A glance out the window to Henry's left showed at least eight inches of snow had piled up while he was lost in a much more exciting, though inconvenient, world.

"I think you're mistaken, Jangle-zee. No one's out on a night like this. No one sane, anyway."

Henry grunted and grabbed at his pounding heart when bells in all sizes and tones sang out as the front door opened.

A man stepped into the lobby, accompanied by a rush of cold air and a whirling fog of gigantic snowflakes.

"Have I died and gone to holiday heaven?" he said. "Is that Bing Crosby and David *Bowie*?"

Henry took a second to focus back on the real world. Sure enough, *Little Drummer Boy* was rum-pum-pumming away.

"It, um, it sure is. Can I help you?"

The man brushed snow from curly blond hair and a reddish beard before turning his attention to broad shoulders covered with green and black flannel. His smile almost outshone the lights in the aluminum tree.

"I certainly hope so. Are you going to tell me this lovely establishment is not only open, but has a vacancy? And maybe even something hot to eat?"

"Well, yeah. All that, a magic cat, and a hot

spring spa. I'm guessing you need a room for the night?"

"In the worst possible way. Wow, The Waitresses, too? And that black tree is the best thing I've seen all day. I love this place already."

Henry got to his feet, grinning at the fact that someone passing through this sleepy town not only loved his tree, but recognized *Christmas Wrapping*.

"Then let me welcome you to the Hidden Springs Inn and Spa. I'm Henry, and that overly friendly kitty at your feet is Zortea. Want me to help bring your bags in now, or are you hungry? Wait, she doesn't like..."

The words died in his throat as Zortea snuggled in the strange man's arms. The rather handsome strange man. She purred loud enough for Henry to hear over the music.

"Zortea, huh? Little Zee? I'm Steve, and you're about the sweetest magic cat I've ever met." He looked up at Henry. "Just show me where the food is, Henry, and I'll help myself. I'm about half-starved."

Henry shook his head, trying not to stare at Steve.

At Zortea. He was trying not to stare at Zortea.

"That's one thing I can't do, leave you to fix your own Christmas Eve dinner. The owners would never forgive me. I honestly think they keep this place so they get to spoil new people rotten all the time. How about this? Come back to the kitchen and tell me what you want, and I'll get it started reheating. Then we'll get your bags."

Steve rubbed his nose against the strangely flirtatious feline's, laughing a wonderful huge laugh when she grabbed at his beard.

"She really *is* a magic cat. Sure, let's check out the food. I've only got one bag I'd need for the night, so no worries there."

Henry took Zortea, and his jaw dropped when she snuggled against his chest, too. What had gotten into Ting-tanglia? He walked back toward the kitchen, hoping his hair wasn't a mess from leaning against the couch for so long.

The kitchen was as plain and industrial as the lobby was holiday fabulous. All stainless steel and stone and top-of-the-line appliances. The only nod to the time of year was a festive set of coffee mugs on the big prep table in the middle, decorated with vivid red poinsettias and candy canes. Henry set Zortea in front of her water bowl and opened the refrigerator that stood taller than he did.

"I'm not supposed to let people come back here, but since it's Christmas Eve and all, I'm hoping you won't report me."

"What a fantastic kitchen," Steve said, looking around. "I won't report you as long as you'll join me for dinner. I was supposed to be sitting down with my crazy family an hour ago, so I really would appreciate it."

Henry started to say he'd eat later, but at the sight of a bowl of mashed potatoes fluffier than the snow outside, his stomach gave out a grumble that just about echoed. After a virtuous and most heroic five seconds, both he and Steve burst out laughing.

"I guess I'd better say yes or my belly will start with the cuss words next."

CHAPTER 4

S teve took in a deep breath and let it out in a long, slow sigh. He'd never admit it to his mother as long as he lived, but that might have been the best Christmas dinner he'd ever eaten.

Rather than messing up the formal dining room for two people, he and Henry had carried as many plates as it took back out to that amazing lobby. Between the incredible decorations, the excellent food, and unexpectedly good company from both his host and the magic cat, Steve's holiday blues had lightened considerably.

Good as the food was—succulent ham and heavenly mashed potatoes and carrots spiced to perfection, just for a start—he'd kept focusing more on the conversation than the demands of his stomach. Now Henry knew about Steve's maddening but good problem of his cyber security work taking off much faster than he'd expected. Steve knew about Henry's excitement and fear of wrapping up his engineering studies and moving on to an apprenticeship.

Childhood stories, grownup disappointments with both of their big, close, and equally loving and infuriating families. The good, the bad, and a little bit of the ugly when it came to dating. Thankfully Henry didn't fall into the complaining about how awful his exes were crap that got on Steve's last possible nerve. Sometimes things just didn't work out.

Finding out that their shared taste in music extended to movies and books, TV and travel. The biggest difference was Steve loved all the trappings and glamour of the holidays as much as Henry claimed to hate it. That twinkle in Henry's eyes when he talked about the decorations surrounding them was impossible to miss, though.

Steve hadn't talked nonstop for two hours to *anyone* for longer than he could remember. Not at work, not back home, and not with that breakup that was starting to feel quite a bit less painful.

A freakish Virginia Christmas Eve blizzard might turn out to be the best thing that had happened to him all year long.

Zortea, otherwise known the sweetest tabby cat in the world, cuddled in his lap again while they waited for Henry to bring out one final bit of dessert.

"I don't know about you, Tab-zanga," Steve said, "but I don't think I can eat another bite."

"Not even if it's fudge?"

Steve couldn't keep himself from grinning at the ceramic plate that looked just like a holiday wreath, piled up with pale brown squares. Henry sat beside him on the couch.

"That's not penuche, is it? I haven't seen that anywhere outside my parents' house for ages!"

"*That's* what it's called," Henry said with that low sort of giggle that was starting to make Steve weak at the knees. "Pen-nu-chi, you said?"

Zortea rearranged herself, chirping the whole time, until she was touching both Steve's leg and Henry's. She started kneading and purring up a storm of her own.

"Well, some of my dad's people up in Vermont say pen-noooch," Steve said. "I'm probably adding an East Tennessee twist. No matter what you call it, it's downright addictive."

He took a bite, humming deep in his throat. Smooth but crisp, with hints of caramel almost like a good praline.

"I didn't think I could eat another bite," Henry

said, closing his eyes as he chewed. "But this is heavenly. I'm glad we had at least one thing you were looking forward to tonight."

Steve decided to listen when his heart said jump, at least to getting a bit flirty. His heart hadn't been paying much attention for the final few months of his last relationship.

Having it speak up again felt pretty damn good.

"Oh, I don't know, Henry. Much as I love traditional Tennessee holidays back home, surprises can be awfully nice, too."

Steve was relieved, and more than a little excited, to see Henry's slow smile and a shy, sexy flush on his cheeks. His full belly managed to move enough to turn warm little loops inside.

"I have to admit I wasn't expecting company at all tonight," Henry said, raising one of his eyebrows. "I'm glad my plans got changed, too."

Steve shifted, trying to move a little closer without being painfully obvious.

"You know, of all the decorations around this place, the one thing I haven't spotted is mistletoe. Seems like a strange omission if you ask me."

Zortea chose that exact moment to jump down and land on the rug with a resounding thump. She looked at Steve, then at Henry, her eyes glowing green from all the Christmas lights.

Then the magic cat trotted out of the lobby with

her crooked tail flipped over her back, chattering and meowing to herself the whole way. Not toward the kitchen this time, but through another doorway off to the side.

"Did we just get scolded by a cat?" Steve said, trying his best not to laugh again.

"That wasn't a scolding." Henry's cheeks flushed even redder, but he was smiling as he glanced toward the doorway. "That was her making a suggestion. She does that a lot. She just ran toward the hot spring spa."

He turned to Steve then, with a half smile that sent the loops in his stomach up toward his chest, and further down. "That's where the mistletoe is, by the way."

"How about you show me that mistletoe?" Steve said. "And maybe join me in the spa?"

Henry leaned a tiny bit closer and shook his head, eyes half closed.

"I really should keep the lobby open. Just in case another lost traveler wanders in."

A buzz in his pocket and against his wrist pulled Steve's gaze away for a second, but after the first few words of the message he was glad of the interruption.

"My mom says they've closed the interstate, more than a foot of snow with more on the way. She's glad I stopped, hopes I can bring my new friend along for dinner when it clears up so they can say thank you for giving me such a warm and cheerful place to stay."

Zortea reappeared in the doorway, flipping her irregular tail back and forth. She let out a high-pitched meow that deepened into a growl that wasn't exactly threatening. Then she ran back the way she'd come.

"I don't care if it *is* a ghost," Henry said, barely loud enough for Steve to hear, before he spoke louder. "Sounds like it's time to close up for the night, then. I'm not about to ignore the magic cat of the inn. Now, about that mistletoe…"

We hope you enjoyed celebrating Uncommon Holidays with us.

For more from Jason A. Adams and Kari Kilgore, turn the page or visit www.SpiralPublishing.net/Anthologies.

ALSO BY KARI KILGORE

I hope you enjoyed reading the stories in *Uncommon Holidays* as much as I enjoyed writing them.

For more stories where speculative elements are either slight or not there at all, head over to www.KariKilgore.com/ContemporaryFiction.

If you're craving more adventures from the Appalachian Mountains, and in many genres from both Kari and Jason, visit www.SpiralPublishing.net/TalesFromAppalachia.

For fantasy of many kinds, be sure to check out www.KariKilgore.com/Fantasy. If you're in a romantic mood, you'll find more at www.KariKilgore.com/Romance.

Be the first to know about release dates and check out more of my fiction, including almost every genre, at www.KariKilgore.com.

Novels:

Until Death

The Dream Thief

Hand Me Downs

Protecting Her Own

The Coffee Bomb and the Corporate Spy

The Great Gold Record Heist

Novellas:

Legacy of the Land

In the Pines

Fantastic Women: A Dark Fantasy Novella Trio

DNA Never Lies

The Box of Possibilities

Murder at the Fabulous Feline Emporium

Team Building Revenge

Dispatches from the Galaxy:

Restricted Species

The Becalmed

Plurapod Pathogen

The Changes Cascade

Near Future Forward (with Jason A. Adams)

Dispatches from the Galaxy: A Space Opera Novella Trio

Dangerous Days on a Pleasure Planet

Storms of Future Past:

Dreaming the Storm

Joining the Storm

Into the Storm

Fighting the Storm

Storms of the Heart

Aunties Among Us

Four-Legged Heroes

Anthologies *with Jason A. Adams*:

Partners in Romance

Shadows Mountain Deep

Partnership in Crime

ALSO BY JASON A. ADAMS

I hope you enjoyed reading the stories in *Uncommon Holidays* as much as we enjoyed writing them.

Visit www.JasonAdamsBooks.com and join the adventure for exclusive new fiction, my past and future travels, and whatever else strikes my fancy. Hope to see you there!

Novellas:

Agonist

Collections and Anthologies:

Normally Fantastic

On the Case!

Capeless Heroes

Through the Squirrel Tree

Tales From the Squirrel Garden: Volume 1

(with Kari Kilgore)

Partnership in Crime

Shadows Mountain Deep

Near Future Forward

ABOUT KARI

Kari Kilgore's wanderlust and imagination lead her all over the world on grand adventures. Her heart and family bring her home to her native Appalachian Mountains of Virginia. From that solid base, she and her husband Jason A. Adams bring those adventures to life in fiction.

Time to read (and write) stories of all kinds brings joy to her winter holidays.

Kari writes contemporary fiction, romance, fantasy, mystery, and science fiction, and she's happiest when she surprises herself. She lives with her husband and fellow author Jason A. Adams, various house critters, and wildlife they're better off not knowing more about.

The Confidential Adventure Club

For Kari's exclusive free After The End stories and deleted scenes, discounts, early releases, adorable pet photos, Kickstarters and other fun projects, Spiral Publishing Exclusive Edition e-books and print books, and a whole lot more not available anywhere else, join us in The Club.

Hope to see you there!

www.KariKilgore.com
www.SpiralPublishing.net
www.ConfidentialAdventureClub.com

BB bookbub.com/authors/kari-kilgore

a amazon.com/author/karikilgore

g goodreads.com/karikilgore

f facebook.com/kari.kilgore.1

ABOUT JASON

Jason A. Adams writes across the spectrum. His stories include science fiction, fantasy, horror, Appalachian folk tales, and romance.

You can find more of his work at www.JasonAdamsBooks.com.

Jason's stories also appear in several issues of *Pulphouse Magazine, Mystery, Crime, and Mayhem, Uncollected Anthology, Thrill Ride*, and WMG Publishing's Holiday Spectaculars.

Jason, a recovering Air Force brat who grew up all over the US and Japan, now perches in the mountains of Southwest Virginia with his excellent author wife Kari Kilgore (www.KariKilgore.com), several spoiled-rotten house critters, and assorted wild visitors from the nearby forest.

news@JasonAdamsBooks.com

ADDITIONAL COPYRIGHT INFORMATION

The Magic Cat of the Hidden Springs Inn and Spa

Originally appeared in *Joyous Christmas: A Holiday Anthology*